Caro could only stare at him. "Tony? Tony's dead."

Incredibly, the man smiled. "Nice try. Where is he?"

"I'm telling you the truth. Tony died over two weeks ago. Check the papers if you don't believe me."

"I saw it. A handy accident is a nice out for a man who'd made Santa Fe too hot to hold him. Maybe the others will even buy that. Not me." He leaned closer, and she fought not to show her fear. "Your husband owes me a hundred thousand. I want it. All of it. From him. Or from you."

She stumbled back a step, trying to find the words that would convince this madman that Tony was dead and that she could no more produce a hundred thousand dollars than she could fly.

"Tell Tony." He moved away, raising his hand in a casual goodbye. "Tell him I'll be in touch."

Books by Marta Perry

Love Inspired Suspense

Love Inspired

MARTA PERRY

has written everything, including Sunday school curriculum, travel articles and magazine stories in more than twenty years of writing, but she feels she's found her home in the stories she writes for the Love Inspired line.

Marta lives in rural Pennsylvania, but she and her husband spend part of each year at their second home in South Carolina. When she's not writing, she's probably visiting her children and her five beautiful grandchildren, traveling, gardening or relaxing with a good book.

Marta loves hearing from readers, and she'll write back with a signed bookmark or a leaflet of Pennsylvania Dutch Recipes. Write to her c/o Steeple Hill Books, 233 Broadway, Suite 1001, New York, NY 10279, e-mail her at marta@martaperry.com or visit her on the Web at www.martaperry.com.

Marta Perry

BURIED SINS

Steeple
Hill®

Published by Steeple Hill Books™

STEEPLE HILL BOOKS

Steeple
Hill®

ISBN-13: 978-0-373-44270-6
ISBN-10:   0-373-44270-X

BURIED SINS

www.SteepleHill.com

Printed in U.S.A.

Draw near to God, and God will draw near to you.
—*James* 4:8

This story is dedicated to my Love Inspired sisters, with thanks for your support. And, as always, to Brian with much love.

ONE

She was being followed. Caroline Hampton pulled her wool jacket around her, fingers tight on the Navajo embroidery, but even that couldn't dissipate the chill that worked its way down her spine.

Santa Fe could be cold in early March, but the shiver that touched her had nothing to do with the temperature. She detoured around the tour group in front of the central monument of the plaza. Ordinarily, she might stop there to do a little people-watching, her fingers itching for a pad and a charcoal to capture the scene. But not when she felt that inimical gaze upon her.

Evading a vendor determined to sell her a *carnita*, she hurried across the square, only half her attention on the colors, movement and excitement that she loved about the old city. She was letting her active imagination run wild; that was all. This persistent sense that someone watched her was some odd aftereffect of shock and grief.

She stopped at a magazine stand, picking up a newspaper and pretending to study it as she used it for a screen to survey the crowd. There, see? No one was paying any attention to her, or at least, no more attention than her tousled mass of red curls and artistic flair with clothing usually merited. Everything was fine—

Her heart thudded, loud in her ears. Everything was not fine. The man had stopped at a flower stand but his gaze was fixed on her, not on the mixed bouquet the vendor thrust at him. Short, stocky, probably in his forties, dressed in the casual Western style that was so common here—he looked like a hundred other men in the plaza at this moment.

But he wasn't. She'd spotted him before—when she was leaving the gallery after work, when she returned to the apartment she and Tony had shared overlooking the river.

This wasn't grief, or an overactive imagination. This was real.

She shoved the newspaper back on the rack, hurrying toward the Palace of the Governors. It was bustling with tourists, its entrance turned into a maze by the Native American craftspeople who spread their wares there. She'd lose him in the crowd; she'd go back to the gallery….

But he'd been at the gallery. He knew where she worked, where she lived. The chill deepened. Her fingers touched the cell phone that was tucked inside the top pocket of her leather shoulder bag. Call the police?

Her stomach seemed to turn at that, emerging memories of the moment they'd arrived at her apartment door to tell her that her husband was dead. To ask her questions she couldn't answer about Tony Gibson.

She wound her way among the craftspeople, nodding

to some of the regulars. Ask them for help? But what could they do? They'd want to call the police.

The knot in her stomach tightened as her mind skirted the older, darker memory that lurked like a snake in the recesses of her mind. She wouldn't think of that, wouldn't let herself remember—

She risked a quick look around. The man was no longer in sight. The tour group, apparently released by their guide, flooded to the crafts vendors on a tide of enthusiasm, swamping everything in their path.

All right. She'd slip around the Museum of Fine Arts and make her way to the city lot where she'd left her car. It would be fine. She rounded the corner.

The man stepped from a doorway to grab her arm.

Caroline took breath to scream, jerking against his grip, trying to remember the proper response from the self-defense class she'd taken last winter.

"You don't want to scream." His voice was pitched low enough to hide under the chatter of the passing crowd. Cold eyes, small and black as two ripe olives, narrowed. "Think of all the questions you'd have to answer about Tony if you did."

"Tony." Her mind seemed to skip a beat, then settle on the name. "What do you have to do with my husband? What do you want?"

"Just the answers to a couple of questions." He smiled, nodded, as if they were two acquaintances who'd happened to meet on the street. "We can stay here in full view of the crowds." The smile had an edge, like the faint scar that crossed his cheek. "Then you'll feel safe."

She summoned courage. Act as if you're in control,

even if you're not. "Or you can beat it before I decide to scream."

She yanked at her arm. A swift kick to his shins might do it—too bad she didn't have heels on today. She'd—

"Just answer me one thing." His tone turned to gravel, and his fingers twisted her wrist, the stab of pain shocking her. "Where is Tony Gibson?"

She could only stare at him. "Tony? Tony's dead."

Fresh grief gripped her heart on the words. The fact that Tony hadn't been the man she thought him, had lied from the first moment they'd met—none of that could alter the fact that she grieved for him.

Incredibly, the man smiled. "Nice try. Where is he?" The fingers twisted again on her wrist—her right hand, she'd never be able to finish the project she was working on if he broke it, she—

Think. Focus. She'd pray, but God had deserted her a long time ago.

"I'm telling you the truth. Tony died over two weeks ago. His car went off the road up in the Sangre de Cristo Mountains. Check the papers if you don't believe me. They covered the story."

With a photograph showing the burned-out car that was all that was left of her month-long marriage.

"I saw it. A handy accident is a nice out for a man who'd made Santa Fe too hot to hold him." He sounded almost admiring. "Maybe the others will even buy that. Not me." He leaned closer, and she fought not to show her fear. "Your husband owes me a hundred thousand. I want it. All of it. From him. Or from you."

He released her so suddenly that she nearly fell. She stumbled back a step, rubbing her wrist, trying to find the words that would convince this madman that Tony was dead and that she could no more produce a hundred thousand dollars than she could fly.

"Tell Tony." He moved away, raising his hand in a casual goodbye. "Tell him I'll be in touch."

Before she could speak he was gone, melting away in the crowd of camera-laden tourists who rounded the corner. She stood, letting them flow past her, forcing her mind to work.

Run. That was all it would say. *That's what you do in a situation like this. You run, you find a new place, you start over.*

As she had when she'd come to Santa Fe. As she always did. She shoved the strap of her bag back on her shoulder and walked quickly in the direction of the car park. She could go north, head for Colorado, get lost in Denver. Or west to LA.

An image formed in her mind, startling her—peaceful green fields dotted with white barns, farmhouses, silos. Gray Amish buggies rattling along narrow roads.

She had a choice. For the first time in years she had a choice. She could choose to run home.

Zachary Burkhalter, Chief of Police, pulled the squad car into his favorite place to watch for drivers speeding through his town. The hardware store shielded him from the view of anyone coming east who was inclined to think the residents of tiny Churchville, Pennsylvania, weren't serious about the twenty-five-miles-per-hour speed limit.

They'd be wrong. One of his charges from the township supervisors was to make sure this isolated section of Lancaster County didn't become a speedway for tourists who were eager to catch a sixty-mile-per-hour glimpse of an Amish wagon or a farmer in black pants and straw hat plowing his field behind a team of horses.

No favors, no leeway, just the law. That was what Zach preferred—a nice, clean-cut line to enforce, with none of the gray fuzziness that so often marred human relationships.

Ruthie, with her mop of brown curls and her huge brown eyes, popped into his head as surely as if she were sitting there. She was almost six now, the light God had brought into his life, and he knew that sooner or later she'd start asking questions about how her parents died. He'd rehearsed his answers a thousand times, but he still wasn't sure they were right. He didn't like not being sure.

A blur of red whizzing past brought his attention back to the present. With something like relief at the distraction, he pulled out onto Main Street in a spray of gravel. He didn't even need to touch the radar for that one. Where did the driver think she was going in such a hurry?

He gave a tiny blare on the siren, saw the woman's head turn as she glanced at the rearview mirror. She flipped on the turn signal and slowed to pull off the road.

He drew up behind her, taking his time. New Mexico license plates—now, there was something you didn't see in Pennsylvania every day. For some reason the image stirred a vague response in his mind, but he couldn't quite place it.

Never mind. It would come. He got out, automatically checking the red compact for anything out of place. The woman's hair matched her car, swinging past her shoulders in a tangle of curls. She had rolled down the driver's-side window by the time he neared it. Her long fingers tapped on the side mirror, as if she had places to go and people to see, and a silver bangle slid along her left wrist with the movement.

Memorable, that's what she was. He sorted through the computer banks in his mind, filled with all the data anyone could want about his township, and came up with the answer. Caroline Hampton, youngest of the Hampton sisters who owned the Three Sisters Inn, just down the road. The one who lived in New Mexico.

"I wasn't speeding, was I?" She looked up at him, green eyes wide.

So apparently they were going to start with innocence. "I'm afraid you were, ma'am. Can I see your license and registration, please?"

She grabbed the oversize leather bag on the seat next to her and began rummaging through it, her movements quick, almost jerky. Irritation, because he'd caught her speeding? Somehow he didn't think that was it.

So Caroline Hampton had come home again. She'd been at the inn at Christmas. They hadn't been introduced, but he remembered her. Any man would—that wild mane of red curls; the slim, lithe figure; the green eyes that at the moment looked rather stormy.

"Here." She snapped the word as she held out the cards.

His hand almost brushed hers when he took them. And *there* was the thing that set his intuition on alert— her almost infinitesimal recoil from the sleeve of his uniform jacket.

Sometimes perfectly innocent people reacted as if

they were serial killers when confronted by the police. It wasn't unusual, but it was something to note.

"How fast was I going? Surely not that much over the speed limit." She tried a smile, but he had the feeling her heart wasn't in it. "I'm afraid I didn't see the sign."

Amusement touched him at the effort. He didn't let it show, of course. He had the official poker face down pat, but even if he hadn't, generations of his Pennsylvania Dutch forebears had ensured that his stolid expression didn't give away much.

"The speed limit drops to twenty-five when you enter Churchville, Ms. Hampton."

Funny. In spite of some superficial resemblance, she wasn't much like her sisters. Andrea, the efficient businesswoman; Rachel, the gentle nurturer. He'd come to know them over the past year, to consider them acquaintances, if not close enough to be friends.

"You know who I am." Those jewel-like green eyes surveyed him warily.

He nodded. "I know your grandmother. And your sisters."

No, Caroline Hampton was a different creature. Jeans, leather boots, chunky turquoise jewelry that spilled out over the cream shirt she wore—she definitely belonged someplace other than this quiet Pennsylvania Dutch backwater.

"I'm on my way to see my grandmother. I guess I got a little too eager." The smile was a bit more assured, as if now that they'd touched common ground, she had a bit of leverage.

He ripped off the ticket and handed it to her. "I'm sure Mrs. Unger would prefer that you arrived in one piece."

The flash of anger in those green eyes was expected. What wasn't expected was something that moved beneath it—some vulnerability in the generous mouth, some hint of…what?

Fear? Why would the likes of Caroline Hampton be afraid of a hick township cop?

For a moment she held the ticket in her left hand, motionless. Then she turned to stuff it in her handbag. The movement to grasp the bag shoved up her right sleeve.

Bruises, dark and angry, even though they'd begun to turn color, marred the fair skin.

"Can I go now?"

He nodded. "Drive safely."

There was no reason to hold her, no excuse to inquire into the fear she was hiding or the marks of someone's hand on her wrist. He stepped back and watched her pull out onto the road with exaggerated caution.

No reason to interfere, but somehow he had the feeling Caroline Hampton wasn't there on an ordinary visit.

"Thank you, Grams." Caroline took the delicate china cup filled with a straw-colored brew.

Chamomile tea was Grams's solution to every ill. Declaring Caroline looked tired, she'd decided that was just what she needed.

The entrance of Emma Zook, Grams's Amish housekeeper, with a laden tray looked a little more promising. One of Emma's hearty sandwiches and a slab of her shoofly pie would do more to revive her than tea.

Rachel hurried to clear the low table in front of the sofa, giving Emma a place to deposit the tray. Since Rachel, her two-years-older sister, and Grams had turned the Unger mansion into a bed-and-breakfast inn, the room that had once been Grandfather's library was now converted into a sort of all-purpose office and family room.

The walls were still lined with books, and Grandfather's portrait presided over the mantel, but the desk held a new computer system. Magazines devoted to country living overflowed a handmade basket near the hearth, and Grams's knitting filled one beside her chair.

Caroline took a huge bite of chicken salad on what had to be fresh-baked whole wheat bread. "Thank you, Emma," she murmured around the mouthful. "This is wonderful."

Emma nodded in satisfaction. "You eat. You're too skinny."

That surprised a laugh out of her. "Most women I know would consider that a compliment."

Emma sniffed, leaving no doubt of her opinion of that, and headed back toward the kitchen and the new loaf of bread she no doubt had rising on the back of the stove.

Grams's blue eyes, still sharp despite her seventy-some years, rested on her in a considering way. "Emma's right. You don't look as well as you should. Is something wrong?"

Since there was no way she could tell just part of the story, she couldn't tell any of it. "I'm fine. Just tired from the trip, that's all. It's good to be here."

"If you'd let us know, I'd have had a room ready." Rachel was ever the innkeeper. "Never mind. It's just good to have you home."

Now was not the moment to point out that this hadn't been home to her since she was six. After beginning her prodigal-daughter return with an encounter with the police, she was just relieved things were going so well with her grandmother and sister.

Her mind cringed away from that moment when she'd heard the wail of the siren. It was not the local cop's fault, obviously, that the sound still had a power to evoke frightening memories. Still, he hadn't needed to give her a ticket. He could have just warned her.

Pay the two dollars, as the old joke went. Just pay the fine, which was likely to be considerably more than that, and forget the whole thing.

Barney, Grams's sheltie, pressed at her knee, and she broke off a tiny piece of sandwich for him and then stroked the silky head. Tiredness was settling, bone deep. She hadn't stopped for more than a few hours all the way back, pushed onward by a panic she'd only just managed to control. That was probably why she'd been speeding when she hit the Churchville village limits— that unreasoning need to be here.

She glanced across the table at Rachel, who was curled up in an armchair, nibbling on a snickerdoodle. Neither she nor Grams had asked the question that must be burning in their minds: Why had she come?

She ought to have created some reasonable explanation during that long trip, but she hadn't. How could she begin? They didn't even know she'd gotten married.

It had seemed like such a sweet idea when Tony proposed it—to wait until they had time to make the trip east and then tell both her family and his in person about their marriage. He'd said his people lived in Philadelphia. Was that true, or was it a mirage, like so much of what he'd told her?

As it had turned out, it was just as well that her family didn't know. If they did, it would be one more reason for them to look at her with the faintly pitying, faintly censoring expression they so often wore.

Poor Caro, the one who's always in trouble. Poor Caro, the one who can't seem to get her life together.

"You look beat," Rachel said, getting up abruptly. "We can catch up on things later. I'll make up a room so you can get settled and take a nap if you want."

Grams stopped her with a slight gesture. "It occurred to me that Caroline might want to have Cal's apartment. Now that he and Andrea are living over in New Holland, it's just standing empty."

Rachel stared at her. "But…won't she want to be in the house? Why would she want to be out in the barn apartment by herself?"

When she'd been here at Christmas, Caro had seen the apartment her older sister's husband had built in one end of the barn where he'd started his carpentry business. It was simple and uncluttered, with a skylight that would give her plenty of natural light for painting. As she so often did, Grams had known exactly what she needed.

"It would be perfect." She interrupted Rachel's argument about her quarters ruthlessly. "Grams, you're a genius. I'd love to have the apartment. If you're sure— I mean, you could rent it to someone else."

"Nonsense." Grams's smile warmed her heart. "It's yours. I thought it would suit you."

Rachel still looked troubled at the idea, but she nodded. "Well, fine, then. It's clean and ready. I'll help you move your things in."

"Great." It seemed to be a done deal. She'd gone

from mindless running to having a home. The thought was oddly disorienting.

Had she really been thinking rationally when she'd packed up what she could fit in the car, arranged to ship the rest, written a note to her boss at the gallery and fled Santa Fe without a backward glance? What would Rachel think if she knew? Or worse, Andrea, the oldest of the three of them, with her sensible, businesslike approach to every problem?

She couldn't explain it, even to herself. She'd just known she couldn't stay there any longer. The urge to run was too strong. The frightening encounter in the plaza had tipped her over the edge, but the need to leave had been building since before Tony's death—probably from the moment she'd realized she'd married a man she didn't really know.

She could only be grateful Grams and Rachel hadn't asked for explanations. She didn't think she could lie to Grams, certainly not under Grandfather's judicious eyes, staring wisely from the portrait. Maybe, somehow, after a little rest, she could figure out what part of the truth she could bear to tell.

The doorbell chimed, startling her. Rachel, already on her feet, headed for the hallway, muttering something about not having any reservations for today.

A low rumble of voices, the sound of footsteps in the hallway. She set down her cup and rose, something in her already steeling. It couldn't be anything to do with her, could it?

The cop—the one who'd stopped her earlier— paused for a moment in the doorway and then came toward them.

"Chief Burkhalter wants to see Caro." Rachel, behind him, looked perplexed. "What…"

She forced a smile. "The chief has already given me a speeding ticket today. Maybe he wants to make sure I'm going to pay up."

Slate-gray eyes in a lean, strong-boned face studied her. "I'm not worried about that, Ms. Hampton." He took a step toward her, and she forced herself not to move back. "Fact is, I've had a call inquiring about you. A call from the Santa Fe Police Department."

TWO

Zach was aware of the sudden silence that greeted his words. The room was so still he could hear the tick of the mantel clock and the thud of the dog's tail against the Oriental carpet.

But there was nothing peaceful about it. Tension flowed from Caroline Hampton. And, to a lesser extent, from her sister and grandmother.

It was a shame they were here, but there wasn't much he could do about that. If he'd come to the door and asked to speak to Caroline privately, it would only have raised more questions.

The plain fact was that something was going on with this woman, and if it had to do with the law, it was his responsibility. And he knew there was something, would have known it even if not for that call from the Santa Fe PD. He could see it in those brilliant green eyes, read it in the tense lines of her body.

"I can't imagine why you'd hear from the Santa Fe police about me. Did I leave behind an unpaid parking ticket?"

He had to admire, in a detached way, the effort it had taken her to produce that light tone.

"Not that I know of." He was willing to pull out the tension just a little longer in the hope that she'd come out with something that wasn't quite so guarded.

"I don't understand." Katherine Unger sat bolt upright in her chair, chin held high. He'd never met anyone who had the aristocratic manner down any better than she did. "Why on earth would the police be interested in Caroline?"

The words might have sounded demanding. But there was a sense of fragility underneath that made it clear he couldn't prolong this.

"Apparently your granddaughter left Santa Fe without telling her friends where she was going. They're worried about her."

Caroline's eyes narrowed. "Are you saying someone reported me missing?"

"Raised an inquiry is more like it. The police department down there was willing to make a few phone calls to allay the woman's fears." He made a play of taking his notebook out and consulting it, although he remembered perfectly well. "Ms. Francine Carrington. I gathered hers was a name that made the police sit up and take notice."

"Caroline, wasn't that your employer at the gallery?" Mrs. Unger glanced from her granddaughter to him. "My granddaughter had a position at one of the finest galleries dedicated to Southwestern art in the state."

She nodded stiffly. "Francine was my boss. And my friend."

"Well, then, why didn't you tell her where you were going?" Rachel looked puzzled. Obviously, that was what she'd have done under the circumstances.

"Because—" Caroline snapped the word and then

seemed to draw rein on her anger. "I left a letter of resignation for her, planning to call her once I got here. I
certainly didn't expect her to be so worried that she'd
call the police."

So she'd left what was apparently a good, success-
ful life at a moment's notice. In his experience, people
didn't do that without a powerful reason.

"Apparently she told the officer she spoke with that
you'd been despondent over the recent death of your
husband. She—"

A sharp, indrawn breath from Mrs. Unger, a murmured exclamation from Rachel. And an expression of
unadulterated fury from Caroline. Apparently he'd
spilled a secret.

"Husband?" Mrs. Unger caught her breath. "Caro,
what is he talking about? Does he have you confused
with someone else?"

Shooting him a look that would drop a charging bull,
Caroline crossed the room and knelt next to her grandmother's chair.

"I'm sorry, Grams. Sorry I didn't tell you. Tony and
I planned to make a trip east this spring, and we were
going to surprise you. But he—" She stopped, her voice
choking, and then cleared her throat and went on. "He
was killed in an accident a few weeks ago."

It was his turn to clear his throat. "I apologize. I
thought you knew all about it, or I wouldn't have blurted
it out that way."

Caroline stood, her hand clasped in her grandmother's.
She had herself under control now, and again he found
himself admiring the effort it took her. "I intended to tell
my family when I got here, but I haven't had the chance."

"I understand." But he didn't, and he suspected Mrs. Unger didn't, either.

"I'm sorry that I worried Mrs. Carrington. I'll give her a call and let her know I'm all right."

There was more to it than that. He sensed it, and he'd learned a long time ago to trust that instinct where people were concerned. Caroline Hampton was hiding something.

She'd left Santa Fe in such a rush that she hadn't even talked to the people closest to her. That wasn't a trip. It was flight.

"I'll be in touch with the department in Santa Fe, then. Let them know you're fine and with your family."

She nodded, eyes wary. "Thank you."

And that was just what worried him, he realized as he headed out the door. Her family.

Mrs. Unger had welcomed her granddaughter with open arms, as was only natural. But from everything he'd heard, she didn't know a lot about the life Caroline had been living in recent years.

It was entirely possible that Caroline Hampton had brought trouble home with her. Someone ought to keep an unbiased eye on her, and it looked as if that someone was him.

Caroline woke up all at once, with none of the usual easy transition from dreams to morning. Maybe because it wasn't morning. She stared at the ceiling in the pitch-black, clutching the edge of the Amish quilt that covered the queen-size bed in the loft of the apartment, and willed her heart to stop pounding.

She'd been doing this for so many weeks that it had

almost begun to seem normal—waking suddenly, panic-stricken, with the sense that something threatened her out there, in the dark. Nothing. There was nothing. There was never anything other than her own haunted memories to threaten her.

She rolled over to catch a glimpse of the bedside clock. Four in the morning. Well, it served her right for getting onto such a crazy schedule. As it was, she'd slept twelve hours straight after that encounter with the cop and the endless explanations to Grams after the man had finally left.

Much as she'd like to blame every problem in her life on Zachary Burkhalter, she really couldn't in all honesty do that. And it wasn't his fault that just seeing him sent her mind spinning back crazily through the years, so that she was again a scared sixteen-year-old, alone, under arrest, at the mercy of— *No.* She jerked her thoughts under control. She didn't think about that ugly time any longer. She wasn't a helpless teenager, deserted by her mother, thrust into the relentless clutches of the law. She was a grown woman, capable of managing on her own. And if she couldn't sleep, she could at least think about something positive.

She shoved pillows up against the oak headboard and sat up in bed. Her new brother-in-law was certainly talented. Most of the furniture in the apartment, as well as the barn apartment itself, had been built by him. Since so much of the furniture was built-in, he'd left it here, and she was the beneficiary.

She couldn't blame Burkhalter, she couldn't blame the comfortable bed, and it was pointless even to blame the stress of the trip. She hadn't slept well in months, maybe since the day she'd met Tony Gibson.

She'd been working on a display of Zuni Pueblo Indian jewelry for the gallery, repairing the threading of the delicate pieces of silver and turquoise, set up at a worktable in the rear of the main showroom. That had been Francine's idea, and Francine had a sharp eye for anything that would draw people into the Carrington Gallery.

As usual, there was a cluster of schoolkids, accompanied by a teacher, and a few retirement-age tourists, in pairs for the most part, cameras around their necks. She'd already answered the routine questions—what did the designs mean, how valuable was the turquoise, did the Pueblo people still make it and, from the tourists, where could they buy a piece.

She gave her spiel, her hands steady at the delicate work as a result of long training. Eyes on her—she was always hypersensitive to the feeling of eyes on her—but she wouldn't let it disrupt her concentration.

The group wandered on to look at something else eventually. Except for one person. He stood in front of the table, close enough to cast a long shadow over the jewelry pieces laid out in front of her.

"Did you have another question?" She'd been aware of him the entire time, of course. Any woman would be. Tall, dark, with eyes like brown velvet and black hair with a tendency to curl. An elegant, chiseled face that seemed to put him a cut above the rest of the crowd. Even his clothing—well-cut flannel slacks, a dress shirt open at the neck, a flash of gold at his throat—was a touch sophisticated for Santa Fe.

"I was just enjoying watching you." His voice was light, assured, maybe a little teasing.

"Most people like seeing how the jewelry is put together." She wasn't averse to a little flirting, if that was what he had in mind.

"They were watching the jewelry," he said. "I was watching you."

She looked up into those soulful eyes and felt a definite flutter of interest. "If you want to learn about Zuni Pueblo jewelry," she began.

"I'd rather learn about C. Hampton," he said, reading her name badge. "What does the *C* stand for? Celeste? Christina? Catherine?"

"Caroline. Caro, for short. And you are?"

"Anthony Gibson. Tony, for short." He extended his hand, and she slid hers into it with the pleasurable sense that something good was beginning.

"It's nice to meet you, Tony."

He held her hand between both of his. "Not nearly as nice as the reverse." He glanced at the gold watch on his wrist. "I have a meeting with Ms. Carrington about the Carrington Foundation charity drive. Shouldn't take more than half an hour. Might you be ready for coffee or lunch by then?"

"I might."

"I'll see you then."

He'd walked away toward the stairs, his figure slim, elegant and cool against the crowd of tourists who'd just come in. Well, she'd thought. Something could come of this.

Something had, she thought now, shoving the quilt back and getting out of bed, toes curling into the rag rug that covered the oak planks of the flooring. It just hadn't been something nice.

She would not stay in bed. If there was one thing she'd learned in the weeks of her disillusionment about her marriage, the weeks of grief, it was that at four o'clock in the morning, thoughts were better faced upright.

She pulled her robe around her body, tying it snugly. She wouldn't go back to sleep now in any event, so she may as well finish the unpacking she'd been too tired to do earlier. She slung one of the suitcases on the bed and began taking things out, methodically filling the drawers of the tall oak dresser that stood on one side of the bed. The loft was small, but the design of closets and chests gave plenty of storage.

Storage for more than she'd brought with her, actually. She'd packed in such a rush that it was a wonder she even had matching socks. Anything she hadn't had room for had been picked up by the moving company for shipment here. When it arrived, she would figure out what to keep and what to get rid of.

Especially Tony's things. Maybe having them out of her life would help her adjust.

She paused, hands full of T-shirts. When had it begun, that sense that all was not right with Tony? Was it as early as their impulsive elopement, when his credit card hadn't worked, and they'd had to use hers? It had grown gradually over the weeks, fueled by the phone calls in the middle of the night, the money that vanished from her checking account, to be replaced a day or two later with only a plausible excuse.

The fear had solidified the evening she'd answered his cell phone while he was in the shower. He'd exploded from the bathroom, dripping and furious, to snatch it from her hands. She'd never seen him like that—had hoped never to again.

Yet she'd seen it once again on the night she'd confronted him, the day she'd realized that her savings account had been wiped out. She still cringed, sick inside, at the thought of the quarrel that followed. She'd always thought she was good in an argument, but she'd never fought the way Tony had, with cold, icy, acid-filled comments that left her humiliated and defenseless.

Then he'd gone, and in the morning the police had come to say he was dead.

She dropped a stack of sweaters on the bed and shoved her hands back through her unruly mop. This was no good. The bad memories were pursuing her even when she had her hands occupied.

She'd go downstairs, make some coffee, see what Rachel had tucked into the refrigerator. She'd feel better once she had some food inside her, able to face the day and figure out where her life was going now.

Shoving her feet into slippers, she started down the open stairway that led into the great room that filled the whole ground-level space. Kitchen flowed into dining area and living room, with its massive leather couch in front of a fieldstone hearth.

She'd start a fire in the fireplace one evening. She'd put some of her own books on the shelves and set up a work table under the skylight. She'd make it hers, in a sense.

She went quickly into the galley kitchen, finding everything close at hand, and measured coffee into the maker that sat on the counter. The familiar, homey movements steadied her. She was safe here. She could take as much time as she needed to plan. There was no hurry.

A loaf of Emma's fruit-and-nut bread rested on the cutting board. She sliced off a couple of thick pieces and popped them in the toaster. She had family. Maybe she'd needed this reminder. She had people who cared what happened to her.

She could forget that sense of being watched that had dogged her since Tony's death. She shivered a little, pulling her robe more tightly around her while she waited for the toast and coffee. She'd confided that in only one person, telling Francine about her urge to give up the apartment, get rid of Tony's things, try to go back to the way she'd been before she met him.

Her boss had been comforting and sympathetic, probably the more so because it hadn't been that many months since she'd lost her own husband.

"I know what I was like after Garner's death," she'd said, flicking a strand of ash-blond hair back with a perfectly manicured nail. "I could hardly stand to stay in that big house at night by myself. Jumping at every sound." She'd nodded wisely. "But what you need is stability. All the grief counselors say that. Don't make any big changes in your life, just give yourself time to heal. And remember, I'm always here for you."

Caro smiled faintly as the toast popped up and busied herself buttering it and pouring coffee into a thick, white mug. Dear Francine. She probably didn't think of herself as the nurturing type, but she'd certainly tried her best to help Caro through a difficult time.

The smile wavered. Except that their situations weren't quite the same. Garner had died peacefully in his bed of a heart attack that was not unexpected. Tony had plunged off a mountain road after a furious quarrel with his wife, leaving behind more unanswered questions than she could begin to count.

And it hadn't been grief or an overactive imagination. Someone had been watching her. She shivered at the thought of that encounter in the plaza. Someone who claimed Tony owed him an impossible amount of money. Someone who claimed Tony was alive.

She hadn't told Francine about that incident. She would the next time they talked. Francine had known Tony longer than she had. She might have some insight that eluded her.

Something tapped on the living room window. She jerked around so abruptly that coffee sloshed out of the mug onto the granite countertop. She pressed her hand down on the cool counter, staring.

Nothing but blackness beyond the window. The security lights that illuminated the back of the inn didn't extend around the corner of the barn.

A branch, probably, from the forsythia bush she'd noticed budding near the building. The wind had blown it against the glass.

Except that there was no wind. Her senses, seeming preternaturally alert, strained to identify any unusual sound. Useless. To her, all the sounds here were unfamiliar.

Something tapped again, jolting her heartbeat up a notch. The building could make dozens of noises for all she knew. And everything was locked up. Rachel had shown her, when she'd helped bring her things in, still worried at the idea of her staying alone. But even Rachel hadn't anticipated fear, just loneliness.

How do you know that's not what it is? You're hearing things, imagining things, out of stress, grief, even guilt. Especially guilt. Tony might be alive today if that quarrel hadn't sent him raging out onto the mountain road.

She shoved that thought away with something like panic. She would not think that, could not believe that.

Setting the mug on the countertop, she turned to the window. The only reasonable thing to do was to check and see if something was there. And she was going to be reasonable, remember? No more impulsive actions. Just look where that had gotten her.

She walked steadily across to the window and peered out. Her eyes had grown accustomed to the darkness, or maybe that was the first light of dawn. She could see the outline of the forsythia branches, delicate gray against black, like a Chinese pen-and-ink drawing.

Her fingers longed for a drawing pencil. Or a charcoal, that would be better. She leaned forward, trying to fix the image in her mind.

Something, some sound or brush of movement alerted her. She stumbled back a step. Something man-sized moved beyond the window. For an instant, she saw a hand, fingers widespread, dark and blurry as if it were enclosed in a glove, press against the pane.

Then it was gone, and she was alone, heart pounding in deep, sickening thuds.

She ran back across the room, fingers fumbling in her handbag for her cell phone. Call—

Who would she call? Grams or Rachel? She could hardly ask them to come save her from whatever lurked outside.

The police? Her finger hovered over the numbers. If she dialed 911, would Zachary Burkhalter answer the phone?

The man was already suspicious of her. That wouldn't keep him from doing his job, she supposed. It wasn't his fault that she feared the police nearly as much as she feared the something that had pressed against the window.

She took a breath. Think. The apartment was locked, and already the first light of dawn stained the sky. She had the cell phone in her hand. He…it…couldn't possibly get in, at least not without making so much noise that she'd have time to call for help.

The panic was fading, the image with it. It had been so fast—was she even sure that's what she'd seen? And if she wasn't sure, how did she explain that to a skeptical cop?

Clutching the phone in one hand, she snapped off the light. Safer in the dark. If someone were outside, now he couldn't look in and see her. She crept quickly toward the stairs, listening for any sound.

Upstairs, she pulled the quilt from the bed and huddled in the chair at the window, peering out like a sentinel. She stayed there until sunrise flooded the countryside with light, until she could see black-clad figures moving around the barn of the Zook farm in the distance.

THREE

In the light of day, sitting in the sunny breakfast room at the inn across from her sister, Caroline decided that her fears had been ridiculous. Already the images that had frightened her were blurring in her mind.

The figure—maybe a branch moving, casting shadows. What she'd thought was a gloved hand could well have been a leaf, blown to stick against the windowpane for a moment and then flutter to the ground. There were plenty of last year's maple leaves left in the hedgerow to be the culprit. Her overactive, middle-of-the-night imagination had done the rest.

"Thanks." She lifted the coffee mug her sister had just refilled. "I need an extra tank of coffee this morning, I think."

"Did you sleep straight through?" Rachel looked up from her cheese omelet, face concerned. "You looked as if you could barely stay on your feet. Grams wanted to wake you for supper, but I thought you'd be better for the sleep."

"You were right." If not for what happened when she woke up, but that wasn't Rachel's doing. Besides, she'd just decided it was imagination, hadn't she?

She'd looked in the flower bed when she went outside this morning. Crocuses were blooming, and tulips had poked inquisitive heads above the ground. The forsythia branches, so eerie in the night, were ready to burst into bloom. There had been no footprints in the mulch, nothing to indicate that anyone had stood there, looking in.

She'd clipped some sprigs of the forsythia, brought them inside and put them in a glass on the breakfast bar as a defiant gesture toward the terrors of the night.

She put a forkful of omelet in her mouth, savoring the flavor. "Wonderful. Your guests must demand seconds all the time. Did Grams eat already?" She glanced toward the chair at the head of the table.

"Emma thought she looked tired and insisted she have her breakfast in bed. When Emma makes up her mind, not even Grams can hold out."

She put down her fork. "Was she that upset because of me?" Because of all the things Caro hadn't told her?

"Don't be silly." Rachel looked genuinely surprised. "She's delighted to have you here. So am I. And Andrea. No, it's just Emma's idea of what's right. You'll see. When people are here, Grams is the perfect hostess, and no one could keep her in bed then."

"It's going well, is it?" Rachel and Grams had started the inn in the historic Unger mansion at the beginning of last summer on something of a shoestring, but they seemed to be happy with how things were going.

"Very well." Rachel's eyes sparkled. "I know people thought this was a foolish decision, but I've never been happier. Being a chef in someone else's restaurant can't hold a candle to living here, working with Grams and being my own boss."

"And then there's Tyler to make you even happier." Her sister was lucky. She'd found both the work that was perfect for her and the man of her dreams. "How is it working out, with him in Baltimore during the week?"

"Not bad." Rachel's gentle face glowed when she spoke of her architect fiancé. "Right now he's in Chicago, but usually he works from here a couple of days a week, while his partner handles things at the office."

"I'm glad for you." Caro reached out to clasp her sister's hand. Rachel deserved her happily-ever-after. She just couldn't help feeling a little lonely in the face of all that happiness.

Rachel squeezed her hand. "I shouldn't be babbling about how lucky I am when you've had such a terrible loss."

"It's all right." What else could she say? Rachel didn't know that the real loss was the discovery that Tony had lied to her, cheated her and then abandoned her in the most final way possible.

That was what happened when you trusted someone. She'd learned that lesson a long time ago. Too bad she'd had to have a refresher course.

She *could* tell Rachel all of it. Rachel would try to understand. She'd be loving and sympathetic, because that was her nature. But underneath, she'd be thinking that poor Caro had blown it again.

It was far better to avoid that as long as possible. She didn't need to lean on her sister. It was safer to rely on no one but herself.

She took a last sip of the cooling coffee and rose. "I'm going to drive down to the grocery store to pick up a few things. Do you need anything?"

Rachel seemed to make a mental inventory. "Actually, you could pick up a bottle of vanilla and a tin of cinnamon for me. Otherwise, I think I'm set. Just put everything on the inn account. Your stuff, too."

"You don't need—"

"Don't argue." Rachel was unusually firm. "If you were staying in the house, you wouldn't think twice about that."

She nodded reluctantly. There was independence, and then there was the fact that her bills were coming due with no money in her bank account, thanks to Tony. *What did you do with it all, Tony?*

She felt a flicker of panic. How could she have been so wrong about him?

Main Street was quiet enough on a Tuesday morning in March that he could patrol it in his sleep. Zach automatically eyeballed the businesses that were closed during the week, making sure everything looked all right. They'd open on the weekends, when the tourists arrived.

The tourist flow would be small awhile yet, and his township police force was correspondingly small. Come summer, they'd add a few part-timers, usually earnest young college students who were majoring in criminal justice.

He enjoyed this quiet time. He liked to be able to spend his evenings at home, playing board games or working puzzles with Ruth, listening to the soft voices of his parents in the kitchen as they did the dishes.

Families were a blessing, but worry went along with that. Look at Caroline Hampton, coming home to her grandmother with who-knows-what in her background.

No matter how you looked at it, that was an odd story, what with her not telling her family she was married, let alone that her husband died. The sort of odd story that made a curious cop want to know what lay behind it.

He'd poked a bit, when he'd called the Santa Fe PD back to let them know that the lost sheep was fine. The officer he'd spoken with had been guarded, which just increased his curiosity.

It might have been the city cop's natural derision for a rural cop, or something more. In any event, the man had said that there was no reason to think the death of Tony Gibson was anything but an accident.

And that way of phrasing it said to him that someone, at least, had wondered.

He slowed, noticing the red compact pulled to the curb, then a quick figure sliding out. Caroline Hampton was headed into Snyder's Grocery. Maybe it was time for his morning cup of coffee. He pulled into the gravel lot next to the store.

When he got inside, Etta Snyder gave him a wave from behind the counter. "Usual coffee, Chief?"

"Sounds good."

Caroline's face had been animated in conversation, but he saw that by-now-familiar jolt of something that might have been fear at the sight of him. It could be dislike, but he had the feeling it went deeper than that.

She cut off something she was saying to the only other customer in the shop—tall guy, midthirties, chinos and windbreaker, slung round with cameras. He'd peg him as a tourist, except that tourists didn't usually travel in the single-male variety, and the cameras looked a little too professional for amateur snapshots.

"Here's the person who can answer your questions," she said, taking a step toward the counter. "Chief Burkhalter knows all about everything when it comes to his township."

He decided to ignore the probable sarcasm in the comment, turning to the stranger. "Something I can help you with?"

The guy looked as if he found him a poor substitute for a gorgeous redhead, but he rallied. "Jason Tenley, Chief. I was just wondering what the etiquette is for getting photos of the Amish. I'm working on a magazine photo story, and—"

"There isn't any," he said bluntly. He'd think any professional photographer would have found that out before coming. "Adult Amish don't want their photographs taken, and it would be an invasion of privacy to do so."

"What about from behind? Or from a distance?"

The guy was certainly enthusiastic enough. "You can ask, but the answer may still be no. Sometimes they'll allow pictures of the children, but again, you'll have to ask."

"And you'd better listen, or the chief might have to give you a ticket." Caroline, turning toward them, seemed to have regained her spunk along with her purchases.

"That's only for speeding," he said gravely. "Although I've been known to ticket for blocking public access, when some outsider tried to take photos of an Amish funeral."

"I'll remember that." The photographer didn't act as if the prospect was going to deter him.

Caroline seemed ready to leave, but they stood in front of the doorway, and he suspected she didn't want to have to ask him to move. Instead she sauntered to the bulletin board and stood staring at it.

"Well, thanks for your help." Tenley glanced at Caroline hopefully. "Goodbye, Ms. Hampton. I hope I'll see you again while I'm here."

She gave him a noncommittal nod, her attention still focused on the bulletin board.

Tenley went out, the bell jingling, and Zach moved over to stand behind Caroline at the bulletin board.

"What are you looking for? The mixed-breed puppies, or that convertible sofa bed? I should warn you that the puppies' parentage is very uncertain, and the sofa bed is one that the Muller kid had at his college apartment."

"You really do know everything about everyone, don't you?" That didn't sound as if she found it admirable. "Neither, but I've found something else I need." She tore off a strip of paper with information about the upcoming craft show at the grange hall.

She turned to go, and he stopped her with a light touch on her arm. She froze.

"I wanted to tell you that I'm sorry for bringing up your husband's death in front of your grandmother. I shouldn't have assumed she already knew about it."

"It doesn't matter." She seemed to force the words out. "I was about to tell her, anyway. If you'll excuse me—" She looked pointedly at his hand on her arm.

He let go, stepping back. *What would you do if I asked you why you're so afraid of me, Caroline? How would you answer that?*

It wasn't a question he could ask, but he wondered. He really did wonder.

* * *

Caroline drove straight to the barn by way of the narrow
lane that ran along the hedgerow. She pulled up to the
gravel parking space near the apartment door and began
to unload. She would put her own perishables away
before running the vanilla and cinnamon over to Rachel
at the house. Maybe by then she'd have controlled her
temper at running into Chief Burkhalter once again.

Arms filled with grocery bags, she shoved the car
door shut with her hip. And turned at the sound of
another vehicle coming up the lane behind her.

It was with a sense almost of resignation that she saw
the township police car driving toward her. Resignation
was dangerous, though. This persistence of Burkhalter's
was unsettling and unwelcome. She'd dealt with enough
lately, and she didn't want to have to cope with an overly
inquisitive country cop.

She leaned against the car, clutching the grocery
bags, and waited while he pulled up behind her, got out
and walked toward her with that deceptively easy stride
of his. If he were anyone else, she might enjoy watching
that lean, long-limbed grace. But he wasn't just anyone.
He was a cop who'd been spending far too much time
snooping into her business.

Her fingers tightened on the bags. "Why are you following me around? Police harassment—"

His eyebrows, a shade darker than his sandy hair,
lifted slightly. "Etta Snyder would be surprised at the accusation, since she sent me after you." He held up the
tin of cinnamon. "She thought you might need this."

Her cheeks were probably as red as her hair. "I'm
sorry. I thought—" Well, maybe it was better not to go

into what she'd thought. "Thank you. That's for my sister, and she'll appreciate it." She hesitated, realizing that probably wasn't enough of an apology. "I am sorry. I shouldn't have jumped to conclusions about you."

Those gray eyes of his didn't give anything away. "No problem. Let me give you a hand with the bags."

Before she could object, he'd taken the grocery bags from her. Snatching them back would only make her look foolish, so instead she fished in her purse for the key.

She was very aware of him following her to the door. Knowing his gaze was on her. The combination of cop and attractive, confident male was disturbing.

"Does Etta often turn you into a grocery delivery-man? I'd think police work would be enough to keep you busy, even in a quiet place like this."

"You haven't been here on a busy Saturday in tourist season if you find it quiet," he said. "Dropping off something you forgot at the store is just being neighborly."

Neighborly. She didn't think she was destined to be neighborly with the local cop. She reached the door, key extended. The door stood ajar. Panic froze her to the spot.

"What is it?" His tone was sharp.

She gestured mutely toward the door. "I locked it when I left." Her voice was breathless. "Someone's in there."

"It doesn't look as if it was broken into. Anyone else have a key?"

She took a breath, trying to shake off the sense of dread that had dogged her in Santa Fe. She was being ridiculous.

"Of course. You're right." Her voice was still too high. "Rachel has a key. She might have brought something over from the house. I'm being stupid."

She stepped forward and ran into an arm that was the approximate strength of a steel bar.

"Probably it's one of the family." His voice was casual, but his expression seemed to have solidified in some way, and his eyes were intent. "But let's play it safe. You stay here." It was a command, not a request.

She opened her mouth to protest and then closed it again. He was right.

He put the bags down and pushed the door open gently with his elbow. She wrapped her arms around herself, chilled in spite of the warmth of the sunshine.

No one would be there who shouldn't be. The things that had troubled her after Tony's death were far away, in a different world, a different life. They couldn't affect her here.

Zach's footsteps sounded on the plank floor, softened when he crossed the braided rugs. She could follow his progress with her ears. First the living room, then the adjoining dining area, then around the breakfast bar into the kitchen. That sound was the door to the laundry room; that, the door to the pantry.

When she heard him mounting the stairs to the loft, she could stand it no longer. She sidled inside. It wouldn't take him long to look around the loft bedroom. Had she made her bed before she left? She hoped so.

Then he was coming back down, frowning at her. "I thought you were going to stay outside."

"This is my home." Brave words, but she wasn't feeling particularly brave.

"There aren't any obvious signs of a break-in. Maybe you'd better check upstairs for any money or valuables you have with you."

She hurried up the steps, brushing against him as she did so, and was a little startled by the wave of awareness that went through her.

She had made the bed, and thank goodness nothing embarrassingly personal was lying out in plain sight. Although Grams would probably find it embarrassing that she'd left things half-unpacked. Grams was a great one for finishing anything you started.

In a moment she was starting back down. "I don't see anything missing upstairs. I was in the middle of unpacking, so it's a bit hard to tell."

And the truth was that neatness had never been her strong suit. Or even a virtue, as far as she was concerned.

Zach stood at the worktable she'd pulled out from the wall, staring at the cartons that held her supplies for jewelry making. She'd wanted those things with her, because it was both a vocation and avocation. Or it would be, if she could ever find a way to make enough money to live on. She patted her pocket, where she'd tucked the information about the local craft show.

He held up a box that contained the supply of turquoise she'd brought. "This must be valuable, isn't it?"

"Fairly. I don't have any really expensive stones. I've been experimenting with variations on some traditional Zuni designs in silver and turquoise." She touched a stone, tracing its striations with the tip of her finger, longing to lose herself in working with it.

"I doubt anybody's been in here with the intent to rob you, or they'd have gone for the obvious."

She nodded, reassured. "Thank you. I—well, I'm glad you were here. I probably overreacted for a moment."

He shrugged, broad shoulders moving under the gray uniform shirt. "A break-in didn't seem likely, but we have our share of sneak thieves, like most places. It's always better to be cautious." His voice had softened, as if he spoke to a friend. "And you've been through a rough time with your husband dying so suddenly."

The sympathy in his voice brought a spurt of tears to her eyes. He was being kind, and she never expected kindness from someone in a uniform.

"We quarreled." The words she hadn't spoken to anyone here just seemed to fall out of her mouth. "We had a fight, and he drove off mad. And in the morning they came to tell me he was dead."

Strong fingers closed over hers, warming her. "It was not your fault. Survivors always think that if they'd done something differently, their loved one wouldn't have died. Don't let yourself fall into that trap."

He had a strength that seemed contagious. She could almost feel it flowing into her. Or maybe she was starting to see him as a man instead of a cop.

"Thank you." She turned away, willing herself to composure. "I appreciate your kindness."

"Plenty of people around here are ready to be neighborly. Just give them a chance."

She nodded, shoving her hair back from her face. Something lay on the breakfast bar—a white sheet of paper that looked as if it had been crumpled and spread flat again. She took a step toward it, recognizing that it was something out of place even before she reached the counter.

She stopped, staring down at the paper, unwilling to touch it. She couldn't seem to take a breath.

"What is it?" Zach covered the space between them in a couple of long strides. "What's wrong?"

She turned, feeling as if she moved all in one piece, like a wooden doll. "That letter." She took a breath, fighting down the rising panic. "Someone has been in here."

Zach grasped her arm, leaning past her to look at the paper without touching it. "Why do you say that?" His tone was neutral, professional again.

"It's a letter my husband wrote to me. I threw it away before I left Santa Fe. Someone came into the house and left it here for me."

FOUR

Zach took a moment before responding. Was this hysteria? Caroline was upset, but she didn't seem irrational, no matter how odd her reaction to that letter.

"Are you sure about that?" Careful, keep your voice neutral, don't jump to conclusions. Getting at the truth was a major part of his job, and he didn't do that by prejudging any situation.

He pulled a pen from his pocket, using the end of it to turn the paper and pull it toward them. "Take a closer look and—"

Before he could finish, she'd snatched up the letter, adding her fingerprints to whatever was already on it. Still, even if what she said was true, returning a letter that belonged to her to begin with probably wasn't a crime.

"I know what I'm talking about." Her voice was tight, and her fingers, when she grasped the letter, showed as white as the paper.

A highly strung person might imagine things after a tragic loss. Her actions in leaving Santa Fe so abruptly weren't what he'd call normal, but she might have reasons no one here knew about. That was what worried him. As well, there were those bruises he'd seen on her arms.

"Isn't it possible this was among the things you brought with you? It could have fallen out when you were unpacking." He glanced toward the stack of boxes that overflowed one of the armchairs. "Maybe Emma or your sister came in, tidying things up, found it and put it there."

That generous mouth set in a firm line, and she shook her head. "They couldn't find something I didn't bring."

Stubborn, and the type to flare up at opposition. Well, she hadn't known stubborn until she'd met a Burkhalter. He could be as persistent as a cat at a mouse hole if necessary. His fingers itched to take the letter and find out what had her so upset about it.

"How can you be so sure it's the same one?"

"Look at it," she commanded. She thrust the paper into his hands, just where he wanted it. "You can see the marks where I crumpled it up before I threw it away."

She was right. The marks were visible, even though the paper had been smoothed out before it was put on the counter. He read quickly, before she could snatch it away again, not that there was much to read—just a single page, written in a sprawling, confident hand. A love note.

Caroline grabbed it. "I wasn't asking you to read it."

"Not many men write love notes anymore, I'd think. Too easy to e-mail or text message instead." And not many women would throw such a message away, especially when the sender had just died. "He must have been thoughtful."

Her expressive face tightened. "Tony could be very charming."

That was the kind of word that could be either praise or censure. "How long were you married?"

She turned away, as if she didn't want him to see her face. "Just over a month."

At that point most couples were still in the honeymoon-glow period. "I'm sorry. That's rough."

She swung back again, temper flaring in her eyes. "You obviously think I'm imagining things. I assure you, grief hasn't made me start to hallucinate. I threw the letter away in Santa Fe. It reappeared here. Now that's real, not imagination, whatever you may think."

"Okay." He leaned back against the granite countertop, taking his time answering. "Question is, do you want to file a complaint about someone entering your apartment?"

"You said the door hadn't been forced." She frowned, the quick anger fading. "I know I locked it when I left."

"The windows are all securely closed now, with the locks snapped." A sensible precaution when no one had been living here, especially since the entrance to the apartment wasn't visible from the main house. "Let's take another look at the door."

He crossed to the entry, and she followed him. He bent to study the lock, moving the door carefully by its edge. The metalwork of the lock was new enough to be still shiny, and no scratches marred its surface.

"I don't see any signs the lock has been picked or forced."

"So only someone with a key could get in."

He shrugged. "Unless it wasn't locked. Easy enough to forget to double check it."

"I suppose." But she didn't sound convinced.

"Look, if you want to file a complaint—"

"No." She backed away from that. "I don't. As you said, there could be some rational explanation."

He studied her face for a moment. "You're not convinced." He wasn't too happy about the situation himself, but he didn't see what else he could do.

Caroline raked her fingers back through that mane of hair, turquoise and silver earrings swinging at the movement. "I'll talk to Emma and my sister. Find out if either of them was in here this afternoon. If not—" She shrugged, eyes clouded. "If not, I guess it's just one of those little mysteries that happen sometimes."

He didn't like mysteries of any size. And he was about to take a step beyond normal police procedure.

"You know, if you were to tell me what made you leave Santa Fe in such a hurry, I might be able to help you."

Her eyes met his for an instant—wide, startled, a little frightened. "How did—"

She stopped, and he could almost see her struggle, wanting to speak. Not trusting him. Or having a good reason why she couldn't trust whatever-it-was to a cop.

"I don't know what you mean." Her voice was flat and unconvincing.

"Neither of us believes that," he said quietly. "I can understand that you don't want to talk to me about your private life, but talk to one of your sisters. Or move into the house, where there are people around all the time."

"I'd rather stay here."

He let the silence stretch, but she had herself under control now. She didn't speak. And he couldn't help her if she wasn't honest with him.

"If you want me, you know how to reach me." He stepped out onto the flagstone that served as a walk.

She summoned a smile, holding the door to close it as if he'd been any ordinary visitor. "Yes. Thank you."

She might change her mind. Decide to tell him about it. But he suspected he was the last person she'd choose to confide in. He just hoped Caroline's secrets weren't going to land her in a mess of trouble.

They were eating dinner around the long table in the breakfast room, but Rachel had made it both festive and formal with white linens, flowers and Grams's Bavarian china. Caroline discovered that the sense of being welcomed home was a bit disconcerting. Nice to know they considered her arrival a cause for celebration, but at the same time, that welcome seemed to call for a response from her that she wasn't sure she was ready to make.

Depend on yourself. That was what life had taught her. Rachel and Andrea were her sisters, but they hadn't lived under the same roof since she was fifteen—longer than that with Andrea. They'd left their mother's erratic existence as soon as they could, as she had.

Andrea and Rachel had left conventionally for college. She was the only one who'd gotten out by way of a correctional facility.

"Great roast, Rachel." Cal, Andrea's husband of four months, leaned back in his chair with satisfaction. "You are one inspired cook. You ought to give the guests breakfast, lunch and dinner."

"No, thanks." Rachel flushed with pleasure at the compliment. "We have enough to do as it is. I'll save my favorite dinner recipes for family."

Andrea nudged her husband. "Haven't I mentioned to you that it's not the wisest thing to praise someone else's cooking more than you praise your wife's?"

"You make the best tuna fish sandwiches this side of the Mississippi," he said, leaning over to kiss her cheek.

Andrea tapped his face lightly with her fingers, eyes sparkling in the glow of the candles. "Sweet-talking will only get you more tuna fish," she warned.

Caro's gaze crossed with Grams's, and she saw an amusement there that was reflected in her own. Marriage had taken away some of Andrea's sharp edges. She'd always be the businesslike one of the family, but Cal had softened the crispness that used to put people off a bit. You could even see the difference in the way she looked, with her blond hair soft around her face and wearing slacks and a sweater instead of her usual blazer.

Had she and Tony ever looked at each other with that incandescent glow? If so, it had been an illusion.

Cal tore his smiling gaze away from his wife. "How do you like the apartment, Caroline? If you find anything wrong, all you have to do is give me a shout."

"Everything seems to work fine." *Except for the fact that someone got in while I was out.* She wasn't sure she wanted to tell them that, wanted to have them look at her the way Zach Burkhalter had, with that doubt in their eyes. "You're obviously a good craftsman."

"He is that," Andrea said. "You have to come over to our new house, so you can see how we've fixed it up. Cal built my accounting office on one end, and his workshop and showroom are in a separate building in the back."

"I'd like to." She could hardly say anything else.

How would they react if she asked how many keys to the barn apartment were floating around in possession of who-knew-who? Would they think she was afraid— the baby sister who couldn't manage on her own?

This was ridiculous. She was a grown woman who'd been taking care of herself for years. There was just something about being back at her grandmother's table that made her feel like a child again.

"You fix up the apartment to suit yourself," Cal said. "That's only right. Maybe I ought to put up a few more outside lights." He nodded toward the wall of windows that overlooked the gardens, lit up now by the security lights on the outbuildings.

More lighting sounded like a comforting idea. "Thanks. I'm careful to lock up, but it would be nice to be able to see a bit farther outside at night."

"Why? Is anything wrong?" Andrea, sharp as ever, jumped on that immediately.

"No. Nothing."

They were family, she argued with herself. She could tell them. Except that she couldn't tell them just a piece of her troubles—she'd have to expose the whole sorry story.

"When you asked if I'd been in the apartment earlier—was it because something happened?" Rachel's voice was troubled.

Andrea's gaze whipped round to her. "You thought someone had been in there?"

"It was nothing." She should have remembered that you could never get away with half truths with Andrea. She'd always taken her role as oldest sister seriously. Far more seriously than Mom had taken motherhood, in fact.

"You had better tell us, Caroline." Grams sat very straight in the chair at the head of the table.

She began to feel like a sulky child, being told to behave by her elders. "It wasn't anything serious. I

found the door ajar when I came home from the store,
and I was sure I'd locked it when I left."

"You probably forgot." Andrea's response had echoes
of childhood—of Andrea bringing the lunch she'd forgotten to school or picking up the jacket she'd left at a
friend's house. *When are you going to be more responsible, Caro?*

"I didn't forget." She could hear the edge in her voice.
"I've been living on my own in the city for years, and
it's second nature to lock up."

"Even so—"

It looked as if Cal nudged his wife under the table to
shut her up. "To tell the truth, I seldom locked up when
I lived there. The latch is probably sticking. I'll stop by
in the morning and take care of it."

"You don't need—" she began.

Cal shook his head decisively. "I'll come by."

His tone didn't leave room for argument, so she just
nodded. Apparently Andrea had found herself a man
who was as strong-willed as she was.

The entrance of Emma from the kitchen put an end
to anything else Andrea might have had to say. Emma
placed a platter in front of Caroline. One look, one sniff
of the delectable aroma, and she knew what it was.

"Emma, your peaches-and-cream cake. That was
always my favorite."

"I remember, ja." Emma's round face beamed with
pleasure. "You'd come into the kitchen and tease me to
make it when you were no more than three."

For an instant she was back in that warm kitchen,
leaning against Emma's full skirt, feeling the comfort
of Emma's hand on her shoulder, the soft cadence of her

speech, the sense that the kitchen was a refuge from tension she didn't understand elsewhere in the house.

"I did, didn't I?" It took an effort to speak around the lump in her throat.

"You'll have a big piece." Emma cut an enormous slab and put it on a flowered dessert plate. "And there is a bowl of whipping cream that I brought from the farm this morning to top it."

Funny. Cal and Emma, the two outsiders, were the ones who made her feel most at home.

But not even their intervention could change the way the others were looking at her. Wondering. Waiting to say it. Poor Caro, always needing to be bailed out. Poor Caro, in trouble again.

"I'm sure we'll find something up here that you can use for your booth for the craft show." Rachel led the way into the attic the next day. She'd been quick to offer her help when she learned that Caroline planned to sell some of her jewelry at the show. "As far as I can tell, no one has thrown anything away in the history of Unger House. They just put it in the attic."

"I see what you mean." She'd forgotten, if she'd ever known, how huge the connecting attics were, and how stuffed with furniture, boxes, trunks and some objects that defied classification. She picked up an odd-looking metal object with a handle. "What on earth is this?"

Rachel grinned. "A cherry pitter. See what I mean?"

"I see that I wouldn't want to be the one to sort all this out."

"We'll keep that in mind." Rachel worked her way

purposefully through a maze of trunks. "I'd vote for Andrea, myself. She's the organized one."

"I doubt she'd appreciate that." She followed Rachel, wondering a little at how easy she was finding it to talk to her sister. The years when their lives had gone in separate directions seemed to have telescoped together.

"Here's the screen I was talking about." Rachel pulled a triple folding screen out from behind a dusty dress form. "This would do for a backdrop, and then you could use one of the folding tables to display your jewelry."

"It's pretty dark. I'd like to find something a little brighter to draw people's attention." She hefted the screen. At least it was easily movable. She'd left most of her craft-show things to be shipped with the apartment's contents, and who knew when the moving company would finally get them here?

"I know just the thing. There are loads of handmade quilts stored in trunks. Throw one of them over the screen, and you've got instant color."

"That would work." It was nice to have Rachel so willing to support her.

Rachel lifted the lid of the nearest trunk. "By the way, did you ever get in touch with your friend in Santa Fe? The one who was worried about you?"

And that was the flip side of support. You owed someone else an explanation of your actions.

"Yes, we had a long talk. I should have called her sooner."

She hadn't, because she hadn't been especially eager to listen to Francine, who had been appalled that Caro had, as she put it, run away.

Well, what else would you call it? That's what you

do. You run away when things turn sour. She'd run from home. She'd packed up and left every time a relationship went bad or a job failed. That was always the default action. Leave.

Rachel, burrowing into the trunk, didn't respond, leaving her free to mull over that conversation with Francine. She'd told Francine what she hadn't told her family—about the man who'd accosted her in the plaza, his demands, his conviction that Tony was still alive.

Surprisingly, Francine hadn't rejected that instantly. "Honestly, Caro, I can't say I knew Tony all that well." She'd sounded troubled. "We worked on a couple of charity events together, and I knew basically what everyone else did—that he was smart, charming, well connected. As for any problems…well, did you think he might have been gambling?"

"That would be an explanation, wouldn't it?" She'd felt her way, trying that on for size. "I never saw any proof, one way or the other."

It was on the tip of her tongue to tell Francine about the disappearance of her own money, but something held her back. Loyalty, maybe, after the wedding promises she'd made. Or just because it revealed how stupid she'd been.

"One thing I'm sure of," Francine said. "If Tony did fake his death in some bizarre need to get out of a difficult situation, he'd find some way to let you know he's still alive. You can be sure of that."

She hadn't found that as comforting as Francine had obviously intended. How could she?

"Caroline." Rachel's voice suggested that she'd said Caro's name several times. "Where are you? You look a thousand miles away." Her expression changed. "I'm sorry. Were you thinking about your husband?"

"Yes, I guess I was." But her thoughts hadn't been what Rachel probably imagined. She went to help her lift a sheet-wrapped bundle from a trunk. "I'm all right. Really." Her mind flicked back to that conversation over the dinner table. "No matter what Andrea might think."

"Oh, honey, Andrea didn't mean that the way it sounded. Don't be mad at her."

"I'm not." She found herself smiling. "You were always the buffer, weren't you? Sometimes you'd side with me, sometimes with Andrea, but usually you were the peacemaker."

"Well, somebody had to be." Smiling back, Rachel began unwrapping the sheet.

The urge to confide in Rachel swept over her, so strong it startled her. She could tell Rachel, because Rachel had always been the understanding one.

But it wasn't fair to ask Rachel to keep her secrets. And she wasn't ready to risk trusting anyone with her troubles and mistakes.

"There." Rachel unrolled the quilt, exposing the vibrant colors of the design. "It's a Log Cabin quilt, one of the ones Emma's mother made, I think."

"It's beautiful." She touched the edge carefully, aware of the damage skin oils could do to aged fabric. "If you're sure you don't mind—"

"It's as much yours as mine," Rachel said. "There might be something you'd like better, though." She pulled out the next bundle, this one wrapped in a yellowing linen sheet. "Goodness, this is really an old one." She squinted at a faded note pinned to the fabric. "According to this, it was made by Grandfather's grandmother in 1856."

"It should be on display, not stored away." The sheet fell back, exposing the quilt. She frowned. "That's an unusual design, isn't it?"

Rachel pointed to the triangles that soared up the fabric. "Flying geese, combined with a star. I don't know enough about antique quilts to have any idea." She folded the sheet back over it.

Caro felt an almost physical pang as the quilt disappeared from view. To actually hold something that had been made by an ancestress almost 150 years ago—had she been as captivated by color and pattern as Caro was? Had she lost herself in her work, too?

"Well, it certainly needs to be better preserved than it is. If you don't mind, I'll see if I can find out how it should be kept."

"Be my guest. That's more your domain than mine." Rachel laid the bundle gently back in the trunk.

Taking the Log Cabin quilt, Caroline stood, stretching. "I'll run this down first and then come back and help carry the—"

Her words died as she passed the attic window. She hadn't realized that from this height she could see over the outbuildings to the barn, even to the walk that curved around to the door of her apartment. And to the flash of movement on that walk.

"Someone's out there." She grabbed Rachel's arm, her heart thudding. He was back. The person who'd been in the apartment was back.

"Who? What?" Rachel followed her gaze. "I don't see anyone."

"Someone was there, by the apartment. I'm not imagining things, and I'll prove it." She thrust the quilt into Rachel's arms and rushed toward the stairs.

FIVE

"I told you not to call him." Caroline glanced from the police car that was bumping down the rutted lane to the barn to her sister.

Rachel looked guilty but determined. "If someone's been prowling around your apartment, it's a matter for the police. I know you had a bad experience—"

"That has nothing to do with it." Rachel didn't know just how bad that experience had been, and she had no intention of telling her. "I suppose it won't hurt to talk to the man, but there's nothing he can do."

Zach Burkhalter slid out of the police car, probably in time to hear what she said. Or, if not, he was quick enough to guess at the conversation based on their expressions. He came toward them with that deceptively casual-looking stride.

"You reported a prowler, Rachel?" He glanced from Rachel to her, as if measuring their responses.

"My sister was the one who saw him. She'll tell you all about it." Rachel turned away, as if leaving.

"Wait a minute." Caro grabbed her arm. She was the one who'd called the man. At least she could stick around for moral support. "You're not going."

Rachel pulled free. "I'd better get back to the house and tell Grams everything is okay. Unless you want to have her out here, that is?"

"Of course not." That was hardly something she could argue, but her sister was going to hear about this later.

"Just tell Zach what you saw. You can trust him. He's one of the good guys." Rachel turned and hurried off around the corner of the barn toward the house.

Caro glanced at the police chief, catching a bemused expression on his face. "You look surprised. Didn't you know my sister thought that about you?"

He shrugged. "Plenty of people don't have good opinions of cops. Like you."

The words dismayed her. Was she really that obvious? "I don't know what you mean."

"Ms. Hampton, I suspect you'd be about as happy to see a snake on your doorstep as to see me. But your sister called me to report a prowler, so I'm here."

She would definitely pay Rachel back for this one. "You'd better come in, but I don't know what you can do."

"Why don't you let me figure that one out."

He followed her inside, and the apartment immediately felt smaller than it should. A police chief, even one in a place as small as Churchville, probably found that air of command useful. She just found it unsettling.

She gestured toward the leather couch and sat down opposite him on the bentwood rocker. "There isn't much to tell. Rachel and I were up in the attic of the house, and I glanced out the window. I hadn't realized that you could see the barn clearly from that height. I saw—"

She hesitated. Had she seen enough to be sure?

"Go ahead." He leaned forward. "Just tell it the way you saw it, without second-guessing."

She nodded. That was exactly what she'd been doing. "I could see the end of the walk that leads to the apartment door. I had a quick glimpse of a figure heading toward the door, but he was out of sight almost before it registered."

"Male?"

She closed her eyes, visualizing. "I said 'he' but I'm not sure. It was just an impression of a human figure, probably male, wearing something dark—maybe a jacket."

The face of the man in the plaza came back to her. He'd worn a denim jacket. Would that have looked dark from a distance?

"Did you see anything else? A vehicle, maybe?"

"No. I ran down the stairs, hoping I could get a look at him. But the dog started to bark, and that could have alerted him. By the time Rachel and I got here, there was no one in sight. And before you ask, it doesn't look as if anyone got inside." She shrugged. "I told you it was a wild-goose chase. That was why I didn't want Rachel to call."

He seemed to have a face designed for expressing doubt. "Did you hear a car when you were running out here?"

"I don't think so." She frowned. "There was traffic going by on the road, but I don't think I heard anything any closer. You're thinking that if there really was a prowler, he'd have had to come in a vehicle."

He seemed to suppress a sigh. "Ms. Hampton, maybe you shouldn't be so quick to assume you know what I'm thinking."

There didn't seem to be anything to say to that. "You seem to be on a first-name basis with my sister."

His gray eyes seemed to lighten with his smile. "I've known her a bit longer. And what I was thinking was that it's not a wild-goose chase if you believe you saw someone who shouldn't be here."

She looked down at her hands, clasped in her lap. "All right. Thank you."

"Still, it makes me wonder." His voice was as easy as if they talked about the weather. "What makes you so quick to decide someone's been prowling around?"

Her hands twisted, tight against each other. He thought he'd boxed her in. "Anyone would think that if—"

He was shaking his head. "You're afraid of something. You don't want to talk about it, but you are."

"That's ridiculous." She forced herself to meet his eyes. "I'm not afraid."

"You left Santa Fe in such a hurry that you didn't even tell your friends where you were going. That looks a lot like running. And if someone's been prowling around here, maybe you had a good reason to run."

She couldn't seem to come up with any rational explanation that would satisfy him and send him away.

He leaned toward her, and she stiffened to keep from pulling back. "Caroline, if you're in trouble, the best thing you can do is tell me about it. Because sooner or later I'll find out what's going on, and it would be better coming from you than from someone else."

She wanted to deny it, but she couldn't. She seemed to be poised on the edge of a high dive, ready to plunge into the unknown. "Someone threatened me."

"When? Where?" He didn't raise his voice, but she felt the demand in it.

"In Santa Fe." She pressed her hand to her head. "The

day before I left there. He'd been following me, and I kept telling myself it was my imagination, but then he grabbed my arm." Something seemed to quake inside her.

Zach reached out, brushing the sleeve of her shirt back. "He left marks."

She looked down at the bruises, faint and yellow now.

"Did you know him?"

"No. I'd never seen him before I noticed him outside the gallery where I worked. And later outside my apartment building."

"So this man you didn't know accosted you. Why didn't you yell for help? Call the police?"

That was what a normal person would do, she supposed. "Because of what he asked me." She took a breath, feeling as if she hadn't inhaled for several minutes. "He wanted to know where Tony was. My husband. And he'd been dead for over two weeks."

"If he didn't know—"

She shook her head. "He knew about the accident. He said that faking your own death was a good thing to do if Santa Fe was getting too hot for you. And that other people might believe it, but he didn't."

"That took you by surprise?"

She stared at him. "Of course it did. My husband was dead. The police told me—showed me pictures of the burned-out car." She had to force the rest of it out. "The fire—there wasn't much left, but I had a funeral."

His face didn't give anything away. He might believe her. Or he might be thinking she was crazy.

"This man. What did he want?"

"He said Tony owed him a hundred thousand dollars." She closed her eyes for a moment. "He wanted it. From Tony or from me."

"Why did your husband owe him the money?" He was relentless. Of course he would be. He was a cop.

"I don't know that he did. I don't know anything about it. I just knew the man scared me and I wanted to get away." She lifted her hands. "I can't tell you what I don't know, any more than I could have told him."

"Okay." He touched her hand in a brief gesture of…what? Sympathy? Or did he just want to calm her enough to get more answers? "Was your husband a gambler?"

"I don't know." She thought of the missing money. If she told him, it would lend credence to the gambling theory.

But she couldn't. She didn't want him, or anyone, to know just what a sham her marriage had been. "I suppose that makes sense. I can't think of any other way he could owe that much."

Zach leaned back, giving her a little breathing room. "So this guy scared you. And instead of going to the police or your friends, you left."

At least he hadn't said "ran away." She met his eyes. "I have family here. With my husband dead, I wanted to be with them."

"I can understand that." But his eyes held a reservation. "So, this man. You're an artist. Can you draw his face?"

She blinked at the sudden change of subject when she'd expected more questions about Tony, more about why she'd left. "I did a sketch right after it happened, but then I tore it up. I'll do another. Would that help?"

"It can't hurt. I can fax it to the authorities in Santa Fe, see what they can come up with. If he's in my territory, I want to know it."

"You think he's the one who got into the apartment." She hadn't expected him to agree with her. "How could he have had access to that letter?"

He shrugged. "The letter might somehow have gotten into the things you packed."

"Or he might have searched the apartment in Santa Fe. Found it in the trash." That made sense. "He'd been outside the building. I saw him."

"Possible." His tone didn't give her a clue as to whether he believed her or not. "About that sketch?"

The thought of him watching over her shoulder while she drew that face tightened her nerves. "I'll work on it and drop it off at your office later this afternoon."

"Fine." He rose. "But you don't need to bring it to me. I'll stop by for it."

If she argued, it would sound as if having him here bothered her. It did, but she'd rather he didn't know.

Of course, he'd probably figured it out already.

"All right." She stood, too, walking him to the door as if he were any ordinary visitor. "Thank you."

"Just one other thing." He paused, holding the door.

She looked at him, eyebrows lifting.

"What he said about your husband. Do you think your husband is still alive, Caroline?"

"No." The word was out, harsh and emphatic, before she thought. She took a breath. "No, I don't."

Zach nodded. Then he stepped outside and closed the door behind him.

* * *

Caroline spread a length of black velvet over the metal folding table Rachel had unearthed for her to use at the craft show. All around her, the cement block fire hall echoed with the clatter and chatter of a hundred-plus crafters getting ready for the event. The doors opened at nine, and everyone wanted to be ready.

The aroma of coffee floated from the food stand at the end of the row. Maybe, once she was set up, she could ask the stall holder next to her to watch the stand while she went for a quart or two of caffeine.

She smoothed out the cloth with her palms and bent to retrieve the first box of jewelry. Silly, maybe, but being here made her feel at home. Veterans of craft shows were a friendly bunch, and Caro had found that no matter what they made, they shared a common bond.

That love of creating something beautiful with your hands was hard to describe but very real. She might not personally understand the drive to make, for instance, the ruffled toilet paper covers that the stand across the walkway offered, but she did know the pleasure of creation.

She began laying out an assortment of turquoise and silver bracelets and necklaces, loving the way they glowed against the black velvet.

"Those are gorgeous." The basket weaver in the next booth leaned over to have a closer look. "I just might end up spending more than I make today. Where did you learn to work with turquoise? Not around here."

Caro shook her head. "Out West. Santa Fe, mostly. The Zunis do some amazing work with silver and turquoise."

"Gorgeous," the woman said again, then grinned and held out her hand. "Karen Burkhalter. Welcome. This is your first time here, isn't it?"

"Yes." She returned a firm grip. Blond hair, hazel eyes, an open, friendly face with a turned-up nose—the woman was probably about her age, she'd guess, with the engaging air of someone who'd never met anyone she didn't turn into a friend.

Burkhalter was a common enough name in Pennsylvania Dutch country. Chances were she didn't even know Zach.

"I'm Caroline Hampton."

"Oh, sure. Your grandmother is Katherine Unger. Everyone knows her youngest granddaughter came home."

"I'm not sure I care for that much celebrity."

Karen grinned. "It's a small township, and most of us have known each other since birth. You'll get used to how nosy we all are about each other's lives."

That was an uncomfortable thought. "You have a great assortment of baskets." She picked one up, admiring the stripes worked into the weaving with different colored reeds. "Is this an egg basket?"

Karen nodded. "They're popular with the tourists, not that any of them are likely to be gathering eggs."

"As long as they buy." That, after all, was the whole point. If she could make a decent amount on the show, she wouldn't feel as if she dangled on a financial precipice.

"The crafters' slogan," Karen agreed. "It's hard to tell whether people will be in a buying mood or not. Usually around here the shows start pretty small, but as we move on into spring, sales pick up."

"If there's a good turn-out—" She stopped, because a familiar figure was headed toward Karen's booth.

Zach Burkhalter. It wasn't a coincidence, then, about the name.

Karen leaned across the table to hug him. "Hey, it's about time you're showing up. I want my coffee."

In jeans and a flannel shirt instead of a uniform, Zach should have looked less intimidating. He didn't.

His gaze shifted from Karen to her, his hand still resting on the other woman's shoulder. His wife? There was absolutely no reason for that possibility to set up such a negative reaction in her.

"Caroline. I didn't realize you were jumping into the craft-show circuit."

"You two know each other, then," Karen said. "I should have known. Being the police chief gives my brother an unfair advantage in meeting newcomers."

"You're Zach's sister." And that shouldn't give her spirits a lift, either. The marital status of Zach Burkhalter was nothing to her.

"The woods are full of Burkhalters around here," Zach said easily. "Mom and Dad each had five siblings, and then they had another five kids to add to the mix."

"You're lucky you just have sisters," Karen said. "Brothers can be such a pain." She threw a light punch toward Zach's shoulder.

"Well, I'd better finish setting up." Standing there looking at Zach was not conducive to her peace of mind. It just made her remember those moments when she'd told him far too much. And had had the sense that he understood even more than she'd told.

Things had been quiet since then. With a little luck, they'd stay that way, and she could stop wondering what had become of that sketch Zach had faxed to Santa Fe.

Caro pulled the quilt from its protective covering and slid her metal chair over next to the screen to climb on.

"Let me give you a hand." Before she could say no, Zach had rounded her table. He took the end of the quilt, lifting it over the screen as she unfolded it. "Is this how you want it?"

"Yes. Thanks." *Now please go away, and let me get back to concentrating on the craft show.* It wasn't Zach's fault that he made her tense up, sure that at any moment he'd say something about the prowler. Or the sketch.

He drew the quilt down behind the screen, and she smoothed it out with her hand. It fit perfectly, falling to table height in a cascade of rich, saturated color.

"That's lovely, too." Karen took a step back to admire the quilt. "Handmade. Are you selling Amish quilts, as well as your jewelry?"

Caro shook her head. "I just wanted it to give me a colorful background. My sister found a treasure trove of quilts stored in the attic."

She started to climb down from the chair, and Zach caught her hand, steadying her. Solid, strong, like the man himself. He wouldn't be a featherweight in a crisis, but she guessed he'd expect a lot from anyone he got close to.

"It's a lot better than looking at cement-block walls," Karen said. "Would you mind if I borrowed the idea and did something similar in my booth?"

"Not at all." She took a step away from Zach's supporting hand. She didn't need support. She did quite well on her own.

"As long as you don't try to borrow the quilt, as well," Zach said.

His sister shot him a haughty look. "I happen to have quilts of my own. Although I'm not sure I have anything as fine as that one." She fingered the stitches, so even and neat that it was hard to believe they were done by hand.

Quilts seemed to be a safe topic of conversation. "Do you know anything about restoring antique quilts? I found one that dates back to pre–Civil War, and I'd love to get it into shape to display."

Karen shook her head. "Not me. The person you should talk to is Agatha Morris. She's a local historian and something of an authority on old quilts and coverlets."

"To say nothing of being the mother of Churchville's mayor, as she'll be sure to point out to you," Zach said.

"You just don't like Keith because he tried to get the county commissioners to cut your budget. And he only did that because you gave him a speeding ticket."

Zach shot his sister a warning glance. "Don't go around saying things like that, Karrie."

She wrinkled her nose at him, in the inevitable manner of little sisters everywhere, and then nodded. "Okay. But how about my coffee? And bring one for Caroline, too. She looks thirsty."

"You don't need—" she began, and then lost track of what she was going to say under the impact of Zach's rare smile.

"Cream? Sugar?" His eyes warmed, almost as if he knew he'd had an effect on her.

"One sugar. No cream." If he kept looking at her that way, she might have to reassess her opinion of him.

Straight-arrow cop, she reminded herself as he sauntered off toward the food stand. Maybe he was one of the good guys, as her sister said, but that didn't mean he could ever understand someone like her.

Zach hadn't intended to spend so much of the day at the craft show. Usually he came by whenever Karrie was exhibiting, just to help her set up or tear down. Somehow today he didn't feel like heading for home.

Ruthie was here, somewhere, with his mother. Mom had been teaching her how to crochet, and that had sparked her interest in Aunt Karrie and the craft show. Thank goodness his daughter had Mom around to handle the girlie stuff. He could teach her how to catch a fish, but he was pretty clueless in some departments.

He rounded the corner of the row of stalls and spotted his sister, leaning across her table to show something to a customer. Beyond her, he could see Caroline, also busy with a customer. Her face was animated as she displayed a bracelet, draping it across her wrist.

His gut tightened at the thought of those bruises on her right wrist. Nobody should treat a woman that way. On the other hand, could he believe her account of how it had happened? He wasn't sure, and until he was, until he knew for sure she wasn't involved in something criminal, he'd tread carefully where Caroline was concerned.

He'd expected to hear something from that Santa Fe PD by now about the sketch he'd faxed them, but so far they'd been silent. His request was probably pretty far down on their priority list.

As he neared the stand, he realized that the person she was talking to was that photographer, Tenley. Interesting that the guy was still around. Something about him hadn't quite rung true from the first time Zach saw him.

Zach picked up one of Karen's baskets and turned it over in his hands, trying to separate their conversation from the buzz of talk that surrounded them.

From what he could make out, Tenley was intent on asking her out, and Caroline was equally intent on selling him something. It seemed to be a bit of a stand-off.

"Are you planning to buy a basket today?" Karen turned to him as her customer moved off, dangling a bag containing one of her smaller items.

"Why would I do that, when you keep giving them to me? If you want your family to buy, you'll have to stop being so generous."

"Small chance of that," Karen said. "You have a birthday coming up, don't you? What kind of basket would you like?"

Caroline, seeming to overhear, turned to smile at his sister. "That's what it is to be related to a crafter. As far as I can tell, my sisters like my jewelry, but they could hardly tell me anything else, could they?"

"Of course they like it," Tenley put in quickly. "Your adaptation of Zuni designs is inspired. As a matter of fact, I'll take the bracelet for *my* sister's birthday."

"Excellent." Caroline beamed. "I'll gift wrap it for you."

"You seem to know a lot about Southwestern design." Zach leaned against the table. "You spend some time out there?"

Tenley looked startled at the direct question, but then he tapped his camera. "My work takes me all over the place. I know enough about Zuni art to appreciate it." He turned quickly back to Caroline, pulling out his wallet. "Don't bother to gift wrap it. I'll take it as it is."

In a moment he'd paid, claimed his package and moved off. Frowning, Caroline turned to Zach.

"You just scared off a customer. I might have been able to sell him something else."

He shrugged. "If someone's scared of the police, it's usually because they have something to hide."

Her reaction to that might have been invisible to anyone else, but not to him. He was looking for it, and he saw it—that faint withdrawal as muscles tightened, the slightest darkening of those clear green eyes. Caroline took that personally. That meant she had reason to do so.

And that meant he should do the thing he'd been putting off for days—run a check on her and find out just what it was about her past she wanted to hide.

"Caroline, here's just the person you should talk with about your quilt." Karen's voice had both of them jerking toward her. His reaction was mild annoyance, but he suspected Caroline's was relief.

The annoyance deepened when he found Agatha Morris and her son Keith standing behind him. He jerked a nod. "Mrs. Morris. Mayor. Enjoying the show?"

Agatha gave him an icy nod before turning to Caroline. With her iron-gray hair worn in a style reminiscent of Queen Elizabeth, her sensible shoes and the flowered dresses she wore whatever the season, Agatha was a formidable figure. "I understand you're Katherine Unger's granddaughter." The words sounded faintly accusing.

Caroline smiled, extending her hand. "I'm Caroline Hampton."

Agatha glanced toward the jewelry, seeming not to notice the gesture, but Keith slid past her to take Caroline's hand. "Welcome to Churchville, Caroline. I'm Keith Morris."

You couldn't fault Keith's manners, even if you did think him too much of a featherweight to be mayor of any town, no matter how small. Maybe the voters had been bemused by the freckles and aw-shucks smile.

"My son is the mayor of Churchville, you know." Agatha never missed an opportunity to mention that. She cast a critical eye at the quilt. "Karen says you had some question about an antique quilt. If it's that one, it's not nearly old enough or unique enough to be of interest."

Caroline seemed to stiffen at the slur. "No, I'm familiar with the history of this one. I found an older quilt in the attic at Unger House, one made by my grandfather's grandmother during the 1850s. It has an interesting design—a combination of flying geese with a star. I'd like to know more about it."

He expected Agatha to welcome the opportunity to show off her expertise. She could be counted on to launch into a lecture at a moment's notice.

But she didn't. She stood perfectly still for a moment, staring at Caroline as if she'd said something off-color. Then she shook her head. "I'm afraid that would hardly be worth pursuing. Such quilts are rather common—of no historic interest at all." She turned away. "Come, Keith."

With an apologetic glance at Caroline, Keith followed his mother down the crowded aisle between the tables.

"Well." Karen sounded as surprised as he was. "I've never known Agatha to miss an opportunity to tell someone exactly how to do almost anything."

Caroline shrugged. "Obviously she didn't think my quilt was worth her time."

Could be. But it was still odd. Odd things seemed to collect around Caroline Hampton, for some reason, and he'd like to know why. Until he did—

"Daddy!" A small hurricane swept toward him, and Ruthie launched herself as if she hadn't seen him for months, instead of hours. "Grammy said you'd be here."

He lifted her in a hug and then set her back on her feet, overwhelmed as he so often was at the way God had brought her into his life. He ruffled her dark-brown curls as his mother came up behind her.

"Ruthie, you shouldn't run off that way." Mom divided a smile among them, sounding a little out of breath.

"Mom, Ruthie, this is Caroline Hampton."

Ruthie caught the edge of the table with two probably grimy hands and propped her chin on it, eyes wide as she looked at the jewelry. "Wow. Did you make those?" Before Caroline could answer she'd ducked down and crawled underneath the table cover, to pop up on the other side next to Caroline, beaming at her. "I love your jewelry. Someday I want to have earrings just like yours."

Smiling, Caroline bent down to let Ruthie touch the dangling spirals of silver that danced from her earlobes. His daughter touched the earring, making it shimmer.

"Ruthie, come out of there now." Instead of waiting

for her to crawl under, he reached across the table and lifted her in his arms. "You know better than to go into someone's booth without permission."

But that wasn't what put the edge in his voice. It was the sight of his daughter leaning against Caroline.

Caroline took a step back, her face paling as if he'd struck her. He was sorry. He didn't want to hurt her.

But like it or not, Caroline was a question mark in his mind. He'd give the woman the benefit of the doubt in any other instance, but not where his daughter was concerned.

SIX

"You really don't need to stay and help me." Caro opened the trunk of her car, peering around the lid at Rachel, who'd walked over from the house to help unload.

"It's no problem." Rachel seized a cardboard box. "Andrea wanted to stop by the show to help out, but she's swamped, with tax time approaching."

Rachel seemed to take it for granted that the family would pitch in to help. A wave of guilt moved through Caro. She hadn't done much in the way of helping Rachel or Grams since she'd been back, had she?

"You have the inn guests to worry about. I'm sure you should be prepping for tomorrow's breakfast or something." She tried to take the box from Rachel's hands, but her sister clung to it, laughing a little.

"Don't be so stubborn, Caro. How many times did I say that to you when we were kids?"

"Pretty often. But not as often as Andrea did." She had to return the smile. "That used to be her theme song when it came to me, as I recall."

"And how you resented it."

Yes, she had. She'd wanted to do things for herself,

but Andrea, always trying so hard to be the big sister, had been just as determined to help her.

Until Andrea had left, headed for college, and she hadn't come back. And then Rachel had taken off in her turn. She could hardly blame them for that, could she? Except that it had left her alone with Mom.

"I'm a big girl now. I've been doing my own loading and unloading from craft shows for a long time—" She looked up, startled, at the sound of another vehicle pulling up behind hers.

Rachel lifted a hand in greeting to Zach as he slid out of the car. "Okay," she said. "I'll let Zach do the heavy lifting, then."

"Glad to," he said, approaching. "Believe me, my sister has me well trained in the whole craft-show routine." He reached past her to begin sliding the folding screen out of the trunk.

Rachel gave her a quick hug. "Come over and we'll raid the refrigerator for supper whenever you're hungry. Grams won't want much after her tea party today." She scurried off, leaving Caro alone with Zach.

He hefted the screen. "You want to get the door?"

"Actually I want to know why you're here. Again." She unlocked the door as she spoke. After all, there was no point in refusing a hand in with the heavy things.

"There's something I need to talk to you about." He stepped inside and set the screen against the wall.

She paused on the doorstep, stiffening. Whatever it was, she didn't want to hear it.

Zach leveled that steady gaze at her. "You look like you're tensed up for bad news."

"I can't imagine that you're here to bring me good

news." She shoved the door shut behind her, aware of the alien scent almost before she registered it mentally. Her head lifted, face swiveling toward the kitchen.

"Coffee smells good." Zach's tone was casual, but his eyes were watchful.

"Yes." She had to force the word out. "But I didn't make any coffee this morning."

He frowned, and then crossed the dining area and rounded the breakfast bar into the kitchen. "Somebody did. The pot's still on—the mug rinsed and left in the drainer. You sure you didn't start it and then forget about it?"

"I didn't make any." She walked to the counter. "I didn't have time."

Her mind flickered to those moments when Zack had brought her coffee at the show. When she'd actually felt as if they were becoming friends. It had been an illusion, like so much else.

"I don't see how you can be sure," he began.

"Because I know what I did and what I didn't do." She snapped the words. "Because even if I had planned to make coffee, I wouldn't have made that kind. Hazelnut. I don't care for hazelnut. I don't have any in the house." Her voice was starting to veer out of control, and she caught herself, breathing hard.

"Who does like hazelnut?" he asked quietly. As if he knew the answer already.

"Tony." It took an effort to swallow. "Tony liked hazelnut. It was all he drank."

He stood for a moment, watching, and then came to plant his hands on top of the counter. "Tony's dead. So how could he be here, making coffee in your kitchen?"

She sank onto the stool, her legs trembling. "He couldn't. He couldn't."

"You said the man who threatened you claimed he was alive." His gaze was so intent on her face that she could feel its heat.

"He was wrong. Or lying. Tony died in that accident. If he hadn't, he'd have come back."

Or would he? He'd already taken everything she had. What else was there to bring him back?

"There's more to it than that." Zach's frown deepened. "That man, the one you drew the sketch of—"

"You've identified him." Her gaze flew to his face. "You know who he is."

"I had a call from the police in Santa Fe. They're familiar with him. His name is Leonard Decker. Mean anything to you?"

She shook her head slowly. "Leonard Decker. I don't remember hearing the name. What was he to my husband?"

"Good question." Zach ran his hand absently along the edge of the granite counter. "According to the officer I talked to, Decker has a finger in a lot of pies, some of them probably illegal. They've never managed to convict him, but he's been under suspicion several times— fencing stolen goods, gambling, that sort of thing."

"Gambling." She repeated the word, her heart sinking, mind flashing back to Francine's speculations about Tony.

"You have any reason to think your husband was involved in anything like that?"

She started to shake her head, but something about that steady gaze seemed to stop her. She didn't trust

Zach. But what was the point of denying something he already seemed to guess?

"There was money missing from my account." She pushed her hair back from her face, aware of the throbbing in her temples. "That was what we fought about, that last night. He'd cleaned out my savings and checking accounts."

"Did he say why he needed the money? Give any explanation?"

"No." His only defense had been in cruel, cutting remarks. "He seemed to think I'd cheated him in some way, letting him believe I had family money when he married me." That accusation had left her numb and speechless. How did you defend against that?

Zach was silent for a moment. Maybe he knew there was nothing safe to say in response to that.

Finally he spoke. "Sounds as if Decker is nobody to fool around with, but I can't see what he'd hope to gain by following you here. Unless he thinks you're going to lead him to Tony."

"Tony is dead." But not even she was convinced by her tone.

"If he isn't, would he contact you?"

"I don't know." Everything she'd thought she knew about Tony had turned out to be a lie. How could she be sure of anything? "Francine—my friend at the gallery— thinks so, but she doesn't know everything."

"You haven't told anyone else about the money."

"No."

She thought he was going to ask why she'd told him, but he didn't. He just shook his head.

"Why not move into the house? Nobody would risk

paying you any surreptitious visits there, to make coffee or anything else."

"That's why." She pressed her palms down on the counter. "Don't you see? If Tony is alive, I have to know. If he's trying to get in touch with me, I have to be where he can reach me."

"Why wouldn't he just walk in, then? Why fool around leaving you hints that he's been here?"

"I don't know. We didn't exactly part on the best of terms. Maybe he's afraid I'm being watched. I don't understand any of it." She squeezed the back of her neck, trying to press the tension out. It didn't help. "But I can certainly understand why you didn't want your daughter anywhere near me."

"Ruthie." His gaze was startled, but she could read the truth there. To do him credit, he didn't try to deny it. "She's my child. I can't expose her to—"

"A criminal like me?"

"I was going to say to someone who might be surrounded by trouble."

"You're a wise parent." If her own parent had been a little wiser, how different might her life have been? She wouldn't have ended up spending those terrifying months in the juvenile detention facility. She wouldn't have carried that around with her for years. Or would she have ended up the same even with good parents?

"I try. Picking it up along the way, I guess. I'd like to help you, Caroline. I'm not sure what I can do."

"There's nothing anyone can do." Anyone except Tony. If he was alive, sooner or later he'd show himself. And then what? Did they try and put the pieces back together again, when there'd been nothing real to begin with?

"Get in touch with me if anything happens that worries you." He put his hand over hers where it lay on the granite, and his grip was warm and strong. Reassuring. "If there's any way I can help you find the truth, I will."

Tears stung her eyes, and she blinked them back. "Thank you. But I don't think—"

His grip tightened. "Promise me. If there's a way I can help, you'll tell me."

There wasn't a way anyone could help, so the promise was a small price to pay to be left alone.

"All right. I promise."

What would anyone have to gain by making Caroline believe that her husband was still alive? Zach drove slowly down the bumpy lane to the main road, his mind still revolving around that odd incident with Caroline.

And the coffee. Was that remotely believable? He came back to the same question. If someone had gone into the apartment while she was out today and deliberately made a pot of her husband's favorite coffee—

It was stretching his imagination to believe that much, but Caroline's reactions had seemed genuine.

So get back to the question. If someone had done that, what would his or her purpose have been? To taunt Caroline about her husband's death? To accuse her, in some veiled way, of contributing to that death? Or to make her think that her husband was still alive?

To think that. Or fear that. He didn't believe for a moment that Caroline had told him everything about that relationship. Had there been reasons why she might have feared Tony Gibson? He hadn't forgotten the bruises on her wrist, and his natural skepticism had made him question her explanation.

Still, the Santa Fe police had identified Leonard Decker, and there was a certain logic that would fit Tony Gibson into the picture with him.

On the other hand, and he had the feeling he was now on his third or fourth hand, Caroline could have engineered the entire story herself. He didn't pretend to be a psychologist, but he'd seen enough human behavior in his years as a cop to know it was seldom entirely rational, especially when driven by strong emotion. If Caroline felt guilty in regard to her husband's death, she might find a way to punish herself through these hints that he was still alive.

He knew a bit about survivor's guilt himself— enough to accept that such a thing could happen, at least. He couldn't forget—would never forget—that Ruthie might not be an orphan if he hadn't failed to do his duty. He ripped his thoughts away from that. This was about Caroline, not him.

There was the least-palatable explanation—that Caroline had set up the situation deliberately, for reasons that had nothing to do with her feelings for Tony. Think about it. What would have happened if Zach hadn't come along just when he did?

Rachel would have helped her carry the craft show things into the apartment, and Rachel would have been the one to hear the odd story about the coffee. She wouldn't have his skepticism. She'd rush to her little sister's defense.

He couldn't dismiss the niggling fear that this could all be part of some elaborate scheme to get money out of Katherine Unger. She'd do anything if she believed her granddaughter needed her help.

Caroline could be telling the exact truth as she understood it, in which case she deserved sympathy and help, not suspicion. But he was a cop, and he couldn't stop thinking like one. In any event, the only way to help anyone, innocent or guilty, was to find the plain, unvarnished truth.

He pulled up to the curb at the police station, glancing at his watch. It was past time he went home for supper, but he had something to do first.

He unlocked the door and went inside. It was just as well that everyone was gone. He didn't want anyone listening to the conversation he was about to have, always assuming he could reach the detective in Santa Fe he'd talked with earlier.

A few minutes later he was leaning back in his chair, listening to Detective Charles Rojas of the Santa Fe PD, who had still been in his office thanks to the time difference.

Rojas seemed to have decided to be a bit more forthcoming. "The thing is, and this is strictly in confidence, Gibson had been under investigation in the weeks before his death."

"Investigation of what?"

Silence on the line.

"Look, someone has been dropping hints to his widow that Tony Gibson is still alive. If through some bizarre chance that's true, it's in both our interests to work together on this." He waited.

A rustling of papers sounded through the phone. "You've got a point there." There was a thud, as if Rojas had propped his feet up on his desk. "Okay, here's the story. Gibson was thought to have been involved in a fairly sophisticated series of scams."

"Thought to be? If he tried to con someone, they ought to be able to identify him."

"You don't know these people." Rojas's voice betrayed his frustration. "Upper-crust society, whatever you want to call them. They don't relish letting the world know they've been made fools of. Seemed like most of them would rather write off the con and forget about it. No one would identify Gibson directly. Maybe, eventually, we'd have pinned it to him, but he drove his car off a cliff first."

"You're sure about the identification of the body?" That was the crux of the matter, as far as he was concerned.

Silence again for a moment. "The car burned badly. Very badly. So far we haven't received complete confirmation as to the driver's identity. But Tony Gibson was seen driving the car about fifteen minutes before it went over the cliff. I think it's a pretty safe assumption that he was the one in the bottom of that ravine."

"If he's dead, who would want his widow to think he was still alive? And why?"

"Good question. And a good reason for you to keep an eye on the Hampton woman. Thing is, she had access to the kind of people Gibson liked to con, through that gallery job of hers. There's no reason to believe she was involved, but there it is. She could have been."

A few more exchanges, and he was off the phone, but he sat staring at it. Rojas had talked because he wanted to keep a line on Caroline Hampton, however tenuous.

If Tony Gibson had been involved in the kind of scam

Rojas suspected, he had been a dangerous man to know. Caroline might be an innocent victim.

Or she might be involved.

He knew more now than he had fifteen minutes ago, but he couldn't say that it made him any happier.

Caroline had never intended to go to church that Sunday. However, she hadn't been prepared to combat Grams's calm assumption that of course she'd go to the worship service at the small church across the road from the inn.

If she'd thought about it, she might have come up with some reason, or rather some excuse, that wouldn't hurt Grams's feelings. As it was, she'd nodded, smiled and tried to close her eyes and ears to the service.

She had a deal with God. He left her alone, and she left Him alone. She didn't want to change that, but she also didn't want to try to explain it to Grams.

The churchyard gate creaked shut as they exited, and she took a breath of relief. It was over, with no harm done. Next Sunday she'd be ready with an excuse.

Grams linked arms with her as they started across the street, Rachel behind them, chatting with Andrea and Cal. "What did you think of the service, Caro?"

Caroline glanced back at the stone church that had stood within its encircling stone wall for the past two hundred and fifty years. The green lawn was splashed with color from spring dresses—in Churchville, people obviously still believed that worship called for their best. In their own way, they were as traditional as the Amish, meeting in someone's house or barn today.

Realizing Grams was looking at her for an answer, she managed a smile. "Nice." That didn't seem to quite cover it. "I noticed Zach Burkhalter with his little girl." She was sorry the moment the words were out. She didn't want to sound as if she were asking about him.

"Not just Zach," Rachel commented as they reached the sidewalk in front of the inn. "I think the Burkhalters have expanded to two pews, haven't they? That was his mother, sitting on the far side of Ruthie."

"I met her at the craft show. And Karen was very helpful." Did that sound stilted? Probably. She hadn't been able to forget the way Zach had snatched his little girl away from her, as if her troubles were contagious.

"They're all helping him raise that child," Grams said. "It's a lovely thing to see."

"He's not married?"

Grams shook her head. "Oh, no. Ruthie is the daughter of some friends he made when he was stationed in the Middle East with the military. The parents were killed very tragically, and Zach adopted her."

She blinked. "I didn't realize." She'd been making assumptions that were amazingly far from the truth.

"She's a dear little thing." Grams smiled. "And so appropriately named. Ruth, finding a home in an alien place."

She nodded, the story from long-ago Sunday school days coming back to her. Apparently this little Ruth had found the place where she belonged, thanks to Zach.

She'd figured him for a straight arrow, but he obviously wasn't the cold fish she'd assumed. She'd seen that when she'd seen him with his little girl.

"I have a casserole in the oven." Rachel headed back toward the kitchen the moment they got inside. "We'll be ready for brunch in a few minutes."

"I'll help you." Caroline followed her to the kitchen, catching the look of surprise that was quickly hidden by Rachel's smile.

Fair enough. She hadn't been much help to anyone since she'd come back, obsessed as she was with her own problems. It was time she changed that.

"What can I do?" She washed her hands quickly and turned back to Rachel, who was pulling a casserole from the oven, her cheeks rosy.

"There's a fruit salad in the fridge that goes on the table. I'll just stick the rolls in to heat up for a minute."

She nodded, lifting the glass bowl from the fridge and removing the plastic wrap that covered the assortment of melon, blueberries, pears and bananas. "Lovely."

Rachel shrugged. "Everything's left over from the guest breakfast. Makes Sunday easier—otherwise I'd never make it to church."

That would suit her. Maybe she could offer to stay behind and make dinner next week, but somehow she didn't think Grams would agree to that.

"Your schedule is pretty tight. I didn't realize what went into running a B & B."

"It's worth it." Rachel's expression softened. "I feel as if I came home when I came back here. Mom certainly never gave us anything that was remotely like a home."

She carried the fruit in and set it on the table. Rachel, following her, took silverware from the massive corner cupboard.

"You and Andrea had more memories from this place than I did. I was too young to have built up much." Was that jealousy she felt? Surely not.

"Doesn't mean you can't start now." Rachel set the table swiftly. "I saw Keith Morris talking with you after service. What do you think of our mayor?"

"Not bad, but his mother tried to freeze me dead with a look. Guess she doesn't fancy me for her baby boy."

Rachel grinned. "She's more likely to snub you for insulting her knowledge of local history."

"On the contrary, I asked very humbly for her advice. About the 1850s quilt we found, remember?"

"You mean she didn't take the opportunity to lecture you on the history of the township?"

"Just said it was 'of no historic interest' and walked off."

"She probably hates that someone else owned it. You ought to talk to Emma's mother-in-law about it. She knows everything there is to know about quilts."

"Who knows everything about quilts?" Grams came into the room, followed by Andrea and Cal.

"Levi Zook's mother. Caro wants to find out more about the flying geese quilt that grandfather's grand-mother made."

Grams nodded. "I think there might be something about it in some family letters your grandfather col-lected. I'll see what I can find."

"Thanks, Grams. I'd like that. I'm not sure why it fas-cinates me so. I actually had a dream the other night about the geese." She'd been flying with them, soaring away from everything that held her back.

"You must have the quilt, since it seems to have touched you," Grams said gently.

Tears stung her eyes, sudden and unexpected. "You shouldn't—I mean, it might be valuable, whatever Mrs. Morris thinks."

"It's yours." Grams pressed her hands. "We'll say no more about it."

She looked from face to face, seeing…what? Love? Acceptance?

Panic swept through her for a moment. She'd told herself that what they thought of her didn't matter—told herself that she was better off relying on no one but herself.

It wasn't true. The longer she was here, the more she became enmeshed in something she'd given up a long time ago.

And the more she risked, when they would eventually let her down.

SEVEN

So that was what Caroline was hiding in her past. Zach had known instinctively there was something.

He leaned back in his desk chair, hearing its familiar squeak, and stared at the computer screen in front of him. It hadn't even been that hard to find—the record of the arrest of the then-sixteen-year-old Caroline Hampton, charged in the robbery of a convenience store in Chicago.

Sixteen. The criminal record of a sixteen-year-old shouldn't be so readily available, but sometimes the legal system didn't work the way it should.

He frowned, leaning forward to read through the report again, filling in the blanks from experience. Two older boys had actually done the crime, roughing up the elderly store owner in the process. Caroline had apparently been the driver, waiting outside.

His frown deepened. She was only sixteen, and she hadn't been inside the store when the crime was committed. A good attorney should have been able to get her off with probation, with her record wiped clean at the end of it. That hadn't happened. Why?

There were only two possibilities that he could see. Either she was far more involved than the bare facts would indicate, or she hadn't had decent representation. Hard to believe that the Unger family wouldn't have hired a lawyer for their granddaughter, but it was always possible they hadn't known. It was the mother who had custody, not Fredrick and Katherine Unger.

He flipped through the text, looking for the resolution of the case. And found it. Caroline Hampton had been confined in a teen correctional facility until her eighteenth birthday.

Pity stirred in him. That was pretty harsh, given her age and the fact that she didn't seem to have been in trouble before. Still, everyone's life wasn't an open book on the Internet. There might have been—must have been—other factors involved.

He drummed his fingers on the scarred edge of the desk. No one had mentioned this serious blip in Caroline's past, at least not to him. Well, they wouldn't, would they?

Still, he'd give a lot to know what the family knew about it. And what they thought about it. Was that a piece of whatever had kept the sisters apart for so long?

More to the point, could it be related to what was happening now? On the surface that seemed unlikely, but he'd learned not to discount anything.

There was a tap on his office door, followed by the creak as it opened. The face of young Eric Snyder appeared. He looked worried, but that meant nothing. Snyder always looked worried, as if he were completely convinced that whatever he decided to do, it was wrong.

As it usually was. He'd never seen anyone with less natural aptitude for police work, but the boy's uncle was a county commissioner, which meant the police force was stuck with him for the moment.

"What is it, Snyder?"

"Ms. Hampton is here to see you, Chief."

Rachel? Or Caroline? Well, he didn't want either of them to see the report in from of him. He saved the file and clicked off.

"Ask her to come in."

A moment later Caroline sidled through the door, looking around as if expecting trouble. "I wanted to see you," she said abruptly.

He stood, noting the by-now-familiar flinch away from him. Well, now he knew why. That aversion of hers to anyone in a uniform could be a sign of guilt. Or it could be the reaction of injured innocence.

"I promised I'd let you know if anything else happened."

"I'm glad you remembered." He reached out to pull his lightweight jacket from the coatrack. "No reason why we have to stay inside on such a nice day. Let's take a walk and talk about it."

Her sigh of relief was audible. "Good." She turned, moving back through the door so quickly that it was almost flight.

He followed, glancing at Snyder. "I'll be back in a few minutes. Take any calls that come in."

The boy gulped, nodding. He didn't like being left in charge of the office. Again, not a desirable quality in a cop.

Caroline was already out on the sidewalk, waiting in the sunshine, hugging her dark denim jacket around her. Under it she wore a blouse that seemed to be made of handkerchiefs sewn together, and her silver and turquoise earrings tangled in her hair.

He joined her, falling into step as she strode away from

police headquarters. "Even warmer than yesterday was. Nice Sunday, wasn't it? Did you enjoy the sermon?"

He'd intended the casual comment to relax her, but it seemed to have the opposite effect. She jammed her hands into the pockets of the denim jacket, her shoulders hunching. "Yes. It made my grandmother happy to have all of us in church with her."

"That sounds as if you wouldn't go on your own."

She shot him a look that bordered on dislike. "That doesn't have anything to do with why I came to see you."

He shrugged. "Just making conversation." But he really did wonder where she was spiritually. It seemed as if Caroline could use a solid underpinning of faith right now. "Sorry. Something else has happened?"

They'd walked past the bakery before she nodded. Reluctant. Caroline was always reluctant when it came to him. He understood that a little better than he had before he'd unearthed the story of her past.

"I got something in the mail." Her hands were shoved tightly into her pockets. "I can't explain it."

He came to a halt at the bench in front of Dora's Yarn Shop, planting his hands on its back and looking at her. The pot of pansies next to the bench gave a bright spot of color to the street. "You plan to let me see it?"

She didn't want to—that much was evident in the apprehension that darkened those green eyes. So why had she come? She was perfectly capable of ignoring that promise he'd screwed out of her.

Maybe she'd run out of excuses. Probably he was the least of a number of bad choices.

She yanked an envelope from her pocket and shoved

it toward him. "This came in today's mail. I didn't know what to do about it."

He took it, handling it by the edges automatically. A business-size envelope, Caroline's name and address printed in computer-generated letters. No return address. The postmark read Philadelphia.

She shifted her weight from one foot to the other impatiently. "Open it."

She obviously already had, no doubt further obscuring any fingerprints that might have survived the handling of the postal service, unlikely as that was. He teased out the enclosure—a folded fragment of copy paper with something hard inside it.

He flipped it open. The briefest of notes in block printing. A small key held fast to the paper with a strip of cellophane tape.

"It's a safe-deposit key," she said impatiently. "I'm sure of it."

He studied the key more closely. "I think you're right. It may be possible to find out what bank it's from, especially if it's in Philadelphia."

"It will be." She stared at the note as if it were a snake. "Tony had family there. Anyway, he said he did. I never met them. Never even talked to them. Tony was going to tell them about our marriage when we came east. That's what he said, anyway."

He nodded slowly, frowning at the words on the page. "Is this your husband's handwriting?"

She took a breath, the sound ragged, as if she had to yank the air in. "I think so."

Black letters. Three short words. She couldn't be

positive from that small a sample, but she probably had a fairly good idea who wrote those words.

"For my wife."

What had possessed her to tell Zach, of all people? He stood there on the sidewalk looking at her, gray eyes intent and watchful, as if weighing every word and gesture. Judging her.

Still, what choice did she have? Who else would she tell?

A brisk breeze ruffled the faces of the pansies, making them shiver, and she shivered with them. The truth was that she couldn't keep this to herself any longer. She didn't know what to do or how to find out what it meant.

She certainly couldn't take this to Grams. And while Andrea's cool common sense might have been welcome, she'd have to tell her everything for the story to make any sense.

At least Zach already knew. She might not be happy about that, but it was a fact.

He nodded, murmuring a greeting to someone passing by. The woman sent a bright, curious gaze Caro's way, and she turned, pulling the collar of her jacket up, as if that might shield her from prying eyes.

Zach folded the envelope and pushed it into his jacket pocket. He took her arm.

"Let's go to the café and have some coffee. You look as if you could stand to warm up. And it won't be crowded this time in the afternoon."

He steered her down the street, turning in to the Distelfink Café. The door closed behind them, and they were enveloped in the mingled aromas of coffee, chicken soup and something baking that smelled like cinnamon.

"See? Empty." Zach led her past several round tables to a booth against the far wall. The tables were covered with brightly painted stencils of the Distelfink, the stylized, mythical bird that appeared on so much Pennsylvania Dutch folk art.

She slid into the booth. The wooden tabletop bore place mats in the same pattern, and the salt and pepper shakers were in the shape of the fanciful birds.

Zach folded himself into the booth and nodded toward the elderly woman who'd emerged from the kitchen. She was as plump and round and rosy as one of the stenciled figures herself. "Two coffees, Annie."

"Sure thing, Zach. How about some peach cobbler to go with it?"

"Sounds good."

She disappeared, and Caroline shook her head. "I don't want any cobbler. I just want to talk about this—"

"If we take Annie up on the peach cobbler, she won't be popping out of the kitchen every two seconds to offer us something else." He turned a laminated menu toward her. "Unless there's something else you want."

She shook her head. The menu, like everything else, was decorated with stenciled figures—birds, stars, Amish buggies. She flipped it over.

"I see they still offer a free ice cream to any child who memorizes the Distelfink poem."

He smiled, his big hands clasped loosely on the table in front of him. "Sure thing. It's a rite of passage in Churchville. You must have done it."

"Oh, yes." Memory teased her. "As I recall, I insisted on standing up on my chair and declaiming it to the entire café. I'm sure I embarrassed my family no end."

"I imagine they thought it was cute. Ruthie's been working on it every time we come in. She'll probably get the whole thing mastered by the next time we're here."

His doting smile told her that he wouldn't be embarrassed by anything his little daughter chose to do.

Annie bustled out of the kitchen with a tray, sliding thick white coffee mugs and huge bowls of peach cobbler, thick with cream and cinnamon, in front of them.

"Anything else I can get for you folks?"

"We're fine, Annie. Thanks." Something in his voice must have indicated this wasn't the time for chitchat. The woman vanished back into the kitchen, leaving them alone.

Caro took a gulp of the coffee, welcoming the warmth that flooded through her. But it wouldn't—couldn't—touch the cold at her very center; the cold that she'd felt when she saw the letter.

Zach didn't pull the envelope out again, and at some level she was grateful. "Have you showed it to your family?"

"No." She thought of all the reasons why not. "I haven't told them much about Tony. Showing them this would mean I'd have to tell them everything. They'd be upset, and I don't want that."

That wasn't all the reason. She knew it. Maybe he did, too. He watched her, the steady gaze making her nervous.

"Your choice," he said finally. "Question is, do you really think it's genuine?"

She stared down into her mug, as if she could read

an answer there. "It looks like Tony's handwriting. I'm not an expert."

"If someone had a sample, it wouldn't be that hard to fake three words."

"I guess not." She pressed her fingertips against her temples, as if that might make her thoughts clearer. "What would be the point of faking it?"

He shrugged. "What would be the point of sending it, even if it's genuine?"

"Exactly." At least they agreed on that. "It's not as if the sender is asking me to do anything. It's just a key."

"Seems like if someone sends you a key, they intend you to use it to open something," he said mildly.

"I get that." She found she was gritting her teeth together and forced herself to stop. "It's postmarked Philadelphia. As I told you, Tony said he had family in Philadelphia."

"That's a link. Still, it's odd, assuming this is from your husband—"

"I don't think we—I can assume that. It could be a fake, or it could be something Tony wrote that someone else sent me."

"Why?"

"I wish I knew." She rubbed her temples again. "Just when I get a line of logic going, it falls apart on me. Why would anyone do any of the things that have happened?"

"Good question." He was silent for a moment, but she felt his gaze on her face. "Should I assume you want to get to the bottom of this?"

"What I want is to be left alone, but it doesn't look as if that's going to happen." *You could run,* the voice whispered at the back of her mind. *You could run away again.*

But she couldn't. At some point, for a reason she didn't quite understand, she'd stopped running. She was here. She was staying. So—

"Yes," she said, surprised by how firm her voice was. "I want to get to the bottom of this whole thing. But how?"

She looked up at him when she asked the question, finding his gaze fixed on her face. For a moment she couldn't seem to catch her breath. He was too close.

Don't be ridiculous, she scolded herself. *He's clear across the table.* But he seemed much nearer.

"I might be able to identify the bank where the safe-deposit box is." He frowned a little. "And with some more information, I might also be able to trace any family he had. What did he tell you about them?"

"Not much." Almost nothing, in fact. Now that seemed suspicious, but at the time, it hadn't surprised her. After all, she didn't see much of her family, so why would she expect something else from him?

"What exactly?" He sounded remarkably patient, and he pulled a small notebook and pen from his pocket, setting it on the place mat in front of him.

She took a breath, trying to remember anything Tony had mentioned. Trying not to look at those strong, capable hands that seemed to hold her future.

"He was named for his father, I know he said that. Anthony Patrick Gibson. He mentioned a married sister once. I helped him pick out a piece of jewelry for her birthday."

Zach scribbled some unreadable notes in a minuscule hand. "Any idea where in Philadelphia? City or suburbs?"

She shook her head slowly. Incredible, that she knew so little about the man she'd married. "I suppose it would all have been in his PDA, but that was in the car with him. I had the impression they lived in the suburbs, maybe on the Main Line."

Nothing definite, she realized now. Tony had managed to convey, just by how he looked and acted, that he'd come from money. Society, the kind of people who learned which fork to use before they learned their ABCs.

Zach raised his eyebrows. "Money?"

"I guess that's what I thought." That was what Tony had thought about her, wasn't it? That Unger House, the grandfather who'd been a judge, the great-grandfather who'd served in the state senate, had automatically conveyed an aura of wealth and privilege.

"Look, we just didn't talk about our families all that much. I suppose, if I'd thought about it, that it was odd I didn't know more, but we were going to see them when we came east. I'd have found out all about them then." She blinked, realization dawning. "But there was an address—there must have been, because the police said they'd notified his family. I don't know how I could have forgotten that."

She'd been numb—that was the only explanation. She'd gotten through those days in a fog of misery, not thinking much beyond the next step she had to take.

"Well, that gives us a place to start, anyway. I'll make some calls and see what I can come up with."

She looked at him, wondering what was really going on behind that spare, taciturn expression. "I…I don't know. Maybe I should just let it drop. I mean, without anything else to go on, how much can I expect to learn?"

He put his hand over hers where it lay on the table, startling her. "Let me tell you what just happened.

You've been stewing about that letter since the mail came this morning, working yourself up until you had to tell someone about it. And then you told me, and saying it out loud relieved some of the pressure. So now you're thinking that it's not so bad after all."

"Are you setting up as a psychiatrist on the side?" She couldn't help the edge to her voice, because he'd nailed it. That was exactly how she'd felt—that pressure to tell someone, that feeling that she couldn't carry it another minute by herself. And then the release, as if by saying the words, she'd convinced herself it wasn't so bad.

"Normal human nature," he said. His fingers tightened around hers. "Don't kid yourself, Caroline. There's something going on here. Something—" he paused, as if wanting to be sure he had the right word "—something malicious about all this. I think we need to find out what's behind it. We, not you."

His gaze was steady on hers. Questioning: Will you let me help you? Will you trust me that much?

She bit her lip. She didn't trust, not easily, and certainly not a cop. But she was running out of options, and Zach Burkhalter was the best choice she had.

Something winced inside her, but she managed to nod. "All right. Will you help me find out what's going on?"

His grip eased fractionally. "Okay. Assuming I can get any answers by then, let's go to Philadelphia tomorrow."

For better or worse, they were committed.

Caroline's hand clenched on the car's armrest, but her nerves had nothing to do with the traffic Zach encountered as he took the off-ramp from the interstate toward the Philadelphia suburb where he'd determined the bank was located.

He shot a sideways glance at her. "Don't you trust my driving?"

"It's not that." She released the armrest and slid her palms down the creases of her lightweight wool slacks. Well, not hers, exactly. The art of dressing to impress a banker was Andrea's style, so she'd borrowed the tan pantsuit from her sister. Even brightened with her favorite turquoise necklace, it didn't look like her.

"There shouldn't be any difficulty accessing the safe-deposit box." Zach glanced in the rearview mirror before swinging around a double-parked car. "You brought all the paperwork, didn't you?"

"Yes." Not only had Zach found the bank, he'd determined what she'd need in order to prove her right to claim the contents of the box. "I'm not worried about that. I was just thinking about how fast you were able to get the information. And how much more of my life must be spread out there for anyone to see who has the skill and the authority."

He glanced at her, his gaze shielded behind the amber sunglasses he wore. "You don't care much for authority, do you?"

That tightened her nerves, but she managed a cool smile and what she hoped was an equally cool tone. "My sisters would tell you that I've always been the rebel."

Whether he wanted to or not, Zach exuded authority. Even today, wearing khakis and a dress shirt instead of his uniform, there was no mistaking that. It was present in the calm gray eyes, the strong planes of his face, the whipcord strength of his long muscles. He was a man who would always take control, whatever the situation.

"You were the one to test all the rules, I guess." He frowned at the GPS system on the dashboard, as if assessing its accuracy.

With their mother the rules had been whatever capricious notion had taken her fancy at the moment, but Caroline had no desire to get into that. "Pretty much. Andrea was the perfect one, of course, and Rachel was the peacemaker. The role of rebel was open, so I took it."

His hand flexed on the gearshift. "I was the oldest in my family. Does that make me perfect?"

"It probably makes you think you are."

"Touché." His glance flickered to her. "Does that rebellion of yours extend to God?"

Her stomach clenched. How had she given so much away to this man that he could even guess that?

"Let's just say I never want to get too close." She hoped he'd let it go at that, but suspected he wouldn't.

"I've felt that way at times, I guess when things were going fine and I thought I could handle everything on my own. Unfortunately in my line of work I get plenty of reminders that I can't, and I have to come running back, looking for help."

She stared out the window, not wanting him to see her face. "And do you get it?"

"Always. But not always in the shape I think it should come."

What about not at all? But she didn't want to hear his answer to that, did she?

The GPS beeped, its metallic voice announcing a

right turn at the next intersection. Zach jerked a nod toward the unit.

"Be nice if God was like that, always alerting you when you were about to make a wrong turn. I guess sometimes you just have to make the mistake first before you're ready to admit it."

"So God stands back and lets you sink." She snapped the words out before she could censor them.

"Was that what you felt happened when you landed in trouble as a teenager?"

She winced as if he'd hit her. So he knew. Well, was that so surprising?

"I take it my so-called criminal record is out there for anyone to see."

"Not anyone." His voice softened, as if he knew he'd hurt her. "The records should have been sealed, given your age, but mistakes happen."

"Don't they, though." And always, it seemed, in someone else's favor. "Well, now that you know, I'm surprised you're helping me. Or maybe you're not. Maybe you're just trying to prove I've done something wrong."

He wouldn't find anything else, no matter how much he searched her past. She'd been scrupulous since the day the gates of Lakecrest closed behind her. No matter how hard he looked, he wouldn't find so much as a parking ticket—nothing to involve her with the police, ever.

Until now. Maybe Zach wasn't dressed like a cop today, but that was who he was, bone deep.

"Look, I didn't want to try and hide the fact that I'd checked into your past. That doesn't mean I'll let it influence my attitude toward you."

Her chin lifted. "As far as I can tell, your opinion of

me was set from the first moment you saw me. This was just confirmation, wasn't it?"

He didn't answer for a moment, occupied with turning into a parking lot. The bank parking lot, she realized, and her stomach churned.

Zach pulled into a parking space and switched off the ignition. Then he turned to her. He pulled off the glasses, and his eyes were intent on her face, so intent that it seemed her skin warmed.

"I'm probably not going to convince you of this, but I came into the situation thinking you're innocent, not thinking you're guilty. Of anything. The fact that you got into trouble as a teenager doesn't have any bearing on anything." He paused, and a muscle twitched at the corner of his mouth. "Except, maybe, that it's made you prejudiced against anyone who wears a uniform, including me."

He didn't give her time to come up with an answer. He just turned and slid out of the car.

EIGHT

"Now, Mrs. Gibson, if you've brought all the proper documentation, I'll just need to have a look at it."

Caroline swallowed hard as she pulled papers from her shoulder bag and handed them to the bank officer. She couldn't stop being aware of Zach, sitting in the chair next to her. Anyone looking at the scene might think them a married couple, applying for a home loan or something else equally routine.

But there was nothing ordinary about this situation. She glanced at the man behind the desk—Dawson, that was it. His name had gone into her brain and fallen back out again as quickly, a tribute to the nerves that seemed to be doing a tango at the moment.

Thin and balding, with a fussy, precise manner, he peered so intently at each document that it seemed the bank itself, with its arched ceilings and echoing tile floors, might tumble down around them if he didn't get this right.

"Mrs. Gibson—"

Her fingers clenched. "Ms. Hampton, please. I kept my birth name."

"Yes, of course." He frowned as if that were, in itself,

a suspicious action. "If you don't mind waiting a few minutes, I'll just need to make copies of these."

She nodded, leaning back in the chair with an assumption of ease. Mrs. Gibson. No one had ever called her that, other than a desk clerk at the hotel where they'd checked in for their three-day honeymoon. She'd never had a chance to get used to the name. Maybe that was just as well.

Zach seemed perfectly ready to wait as long as it took. He had a gift of stillness, and for an instant her fingers itched for a pad and pencil to capture that.

But if she did, what would it say about the man? The ease of his long body in the chair, the carefully neutral expression on his face—everything about Zach seemed designed to camouflage his emotions, assuming he had any.

Well, of course he did. She was being ridiculous. She'd seen him with his daughter, and there was certainly no lack of feeling there. The fact that he wore that shuttered look with her just confirmed that he saw her as part of his job, nothing else.

He knew about her past. She still had difficulty swallowing that. To do him justice, he hadn't let that prejudice him against her, but she suspected it had to weigh in the balance he kept in his mind, with each new fact he learned about her being dropped on the scale.

He didn't know everything. Her stomach twisted. He couldn't. The ugliest thing about that time would never appear in any official report, even though it had left an indelible stain on her life.

She straightened her back, clasping her hands loosely in her lap and trying to behave as she imagined Andrea would in such a situation—cool, confident, perfectly at ease.

"He's been gone a long time." The words came out before she could tell herself that saying them made her sound anything but cool and confident. "Maybe he found something wrong."

The faintest of frowns made a crease between Zach's level eyebrows. "What could he find wrong?"

"Nothing. Nothing at all." She'd say she was just nervous, but that was probably pretty obvious to him. "I…I don't like this."

"Why?" He leaned forward, his gaze probing.

"I just feel that way. Does there have to be a reason?"

He considered that calmly. "There usually is."

She clamped her mouth shut to keep from snapping at him. She counted to ten. "All right." Maybe she should have made it twenty. "I guess it bothers me to feel that I'm being manipulated. That I'm doing exactly what someone wants me to."

To her surprise, he nodded. "I understand. And you're probably right, but what other choice did you have?"

"None." Unfortunately, he was right, too. "That doesn't mean I have to like it."

"I'd say the best thing would be to move cautiously. No matter what is in that box, you don't have to act on it today."

"Right." She took a deep breath and tried a smile. "You're right. Whatever it is, I don't have to rush into dealing with it."

Dawson came toward them, sliding papers into a file. "Here are your originals back, Mrs.—Ms. Hampton."

He handed them to her. "Naturally, I'd like to express our sympathy in your loss."

"Thank you."

"As you probably know, Pennsylvania law requires that a safe-deposit box be sealed upon the death of the owner until it can be inventoried by a representative of the Department of Revenue."

"No, I didn't know that." If she had, she wouldn't be here. What was the point of this exercise, if she couldn't access the box?

"However, since you and your husband rented the box jointly, that's not an issue. If you'll just come along, I'll get the box out for you."

Jointly. She felt as if she'd stepped onstage in a play where she didn't know the lines. She hadn't rented the box—at least not knowingly. But the bank officer clearly thought she had.

And Zach—what did he think? Did he assume she'd been lying all along about this?

Moving automatically, she followed the man, aware of Zach, close on her heels. Down one long hall, footsteps echoing on the tile, and then a flight of stairs. Dawson led them into a small room lined with storage compartments, its only furniture a table in the center of the room. Obviously the bank didn't encourage its patrons to hang around here.

Murmuring the number under his breath, Dawson retrieved the box, placing it on the table. Once it was unlocked, he stepped back with a suggestion of duty fulfilled.

"There you are. I'll wait until you're finished."

She was barely aware of the man moving to the

doorway, turning his back as if to give them some semblance of privacy. All her attention was focused on the box. On the feeling it aroused.

Dread. There was no other word for it. Whatever Tony had put in that safe-deposit box, she didn't want to know. And however he'd gotten her name on the box, she didn't want to know that, either.

"Would you like me to wait outside?" Zach said.

She shook her head slowly. "No. Stay. Whatever it is, I think I'd like a witness." Besides, if she didn't let him stay, that would simply make him more suspicious.

"If that's what you want."

He was probably pleased. He saw this as one more step toward solving a puzzle, nothing more.

She couldn't be that detached. Tony's secrets hadn't died with him, and she was about to see one of them. Somehow she didn't think it could be anything good.

She reached out, her hands a little unsteady, and lifted the lid from the box. It clattered when she dropped it back onto the table. She heard a swift intake of breath from Zach.

She didn't seem to be breathing at all. She took an involuntary step back, not wanting to admit what she was seeing.

Money. The safe-deposit box was stuffed to the brim with cash.

Zach leaned against the back of the park bench, trying to look anything but as tense as he felt. Caroline was upset enough already. The last thing she needed was for him to add to that.

She sat on the other end of the concrete-and-redwood

bench, staring out over the wide, placid river, as if intent on the rowing sculls that zipped along its surface like water bugs. But her hands clasped each other so tightly that the knuckles were white, and even the warmth of the spring sunshine didn't keep the occasional shiver from going through her.

"Have a little more of your coffee," he urged.

She lifted the foam cup to her lips and drank without looking at it. When they'd finally gotten out of the bank he'd wanted to find a restaurant where they could sit and talk, but she'd just kept shaking her head.

Well, he could understand why she didn't want to feel hemmed in. He'd finally gone through a fast-food drive-through and ordered her a large coffee with sugar. Something hot and sweet seemed the right remedy for shock.

Was the shock genuine? The analytical part of his cop's brain weighed her reactions. She'd certainly acted surprised when Dawson had pulled out the rental lease with her name on it. To suppose that she'd already known about the box was to imagine she'd been taking him for a ride all along, and he didn't think he was that gullible.

And she couldn't have mimicked that shock when she'd flipped the box lid back and seen the money. Whatever she'd expected to find in that safe-deposit box, it wasn't that.

"You feel like talking about it now?" He edged a little closer, even though there was no one within earshot.

The ground sloped gently from where they sat down to the river, and the few people who were in the park at this hour were on the paved path that led along the water— a couple of joggers, a couple of women pushing strollers.

Caroline lifted her hand, palm up. "I don't know what to say. I don't understand any of it."

"You didn't have any idea Tony had rented that safe-deposit box in your names?"

She shook her head, the movement setting her dangling silver earrings dancing. "No. I didn't even know he'd been in Philadelphia. Why wouldn't he tell me that? I wouldn't have found it suspicious if he'd said he had to go there on business."

Some people lied even when it would be easier to tell the truth, but it seemed pointless to say so. "The rental form had what looked like your signature on it."

She rubbed her forehead. "I guess it's faintly possible that he slipped the form in with some other papers to sign, and I didn't notice what it was."

She didn't sound convinced. Well, he wasn't, either. Caroline might be something of a free spirit, maybe a tad irresponsible, but he doubted she'd sign something without even looking at it.

"And the money? You didn't know he had that much salted away?"

Nearly two hundred thousand dollars. Caroline had refused to so much as touch the contents of the box, but finally she'd agreed to let him count it.

Afterward, he'd put the cash back into the box, and Caroline had returned it to the bank's care. What else was there to do? If it hadn't been for Caroline's name on that lease, the bank officer would have sealed the box himself, not letting them do anything but look for a will until someone was present from the Department of Revenue.

Caroline transferred her gaze from the sculls to him. "It's not my money."

She'd been saying that, in one variation or another, since they'd left the bank.

"If it belonged to your husband, then it belongs to you, unless he made a will leaving it elsewhere."

"As far as I know, Tony didn't make a will. But then, there's a lot that I don't know, obviously." Her voice held an edge.

"Barring a will, it would go to you as next of kin."

"I don't want it." The suppressed emotion in her voice startled him. "Even if it did belong to Tony, I can't imagine that he came by it honestly."

"You said he took money out of your account. You could probably legitimately claim that, even if—"

He stopped, because she was shaking her head. "I don't want it, I tell you. I just want to forget I ever saw it."

Her voice had the ring of truth. She had to be hard up for money, if Gibson really had cleaned her out, but she seemed adamant about that.

"I can understand, I guess," he said slowly, "but I don't think you're going to be able to do that. Seems to me you ought to notify the Santa Fe police."

Fear flared in those green eyes. "No! I mean, I don't want to have anything to do with it."

Anything to do with the police—that was what she meant. He hated to push her. What he wanted to do was put his arm around her shoulder, pull her close and tell her everything was going to be all right.

But he couldn't. It wouldn't be professional, for one thing. And he couldn't promise things were going to be fine. His instincts told him a law had been violated somewhere in all of this, even if he couldn't put his finger on it yet.

"Where do you think the money came from?" Maybe if he could get her thinking, the fear would leave her eyes and they could talk about notifying the police in a rational manner.

"I don't know." She rubbed the sleeves of her suit jacket. "Based on when he rented the safe-deposit box, it was several months ago. I just can't imagine, but obviously I didn't have a clue about his finances."

"What about gambling winnings?"

She winced a little, but she kept her back ramrod straight, reminding him of her grandmother. "I guess that's one possibility."

She clearly didn't want to admit that, but it seemed the obvious answer to a lot of the problems she'd been having. A compulsive gambler, losing money he couldn't repay, might resort to stealing from his wife or even driving his car off the side of a mountain.

The trouble with that scenario was that it didn't fit the facts. Tony, with a safe-deposit box stuffed with cash, didn't look like any loser he'd ever seen.

He studied Caroline's face. Those normally clear green eyes were clouded, the shadows under them looking like bruises on the fair skin. There were lines of strain around her generous mouth, and he had the sense that she was hanging on to her composure by a thread.

Sooner or later, information about the money would have to be passed on to the Santa Fe police. Since Tony's death wasn't being investigated, he didn't feel an urgency to do it today.

He could give Caroline another day, maybe. But if she hadn't decided by then to talk to the New Mexico cops, he'd have to do it.

"Do you want to head home now?" He planted his hand on the top slat of the bench, ready to get up.

She looked up, startled. "We're going to try and find Tony's family, aren't we? You said that you had a possible address."

"I do. But I thought maybe you'd had enough for one day."

She managed a smile. "Think how offended my grandmother would be at the idea that an Unger wouldn't do her duty, no matter what."

"You don't have to prove anything, Caroline." But maybe, in her mind, she did.

She rose, slinging the strap of her leather bag on her shoulder. "I'd rather get it over with. If Tony has family here in Philadelphia, I think it's time I met them."

"Are you sure this is the right address?" Caroline stared through the windshield. The row house, its brick faded and stained, sat behind its wire mesh fence with an air of cringing away from the street. Small wonder. This wasn't the worst neighborhood in Philadelphia, but it had an air of having come down in the world considerably in recent years.

Zach consulted the address in his notebook, checked the GPS monitor and nodded. "This is it, all right. Not what you expected?"

"No. I can't imagine Tony growing up here." She thought of the safe-deposit box stuffed with money, and her stomach tightened. "But I seem to have been wrong about plenty of things where Tony was concerned."

Tony, who were you? Was there anything real about our marriage?

The look Zach sent her seemed to assess her stability. "Are you sure you want to do this now?"

She took a deep breath. In a situation like this, her grandmother would rely on her faith. For a moment she felt a twinge of something that might be envy. To feel that Someone was always there—

But she couldn't. She grabbed the door handle. "Let's go."

"Wait a second." He reached across her to clasp her hand before she could open the door. For a moment she couldn't seem to breathe. He was too close, much too close. She could smell the clean scent of his soap, feel the hard muscles in the arm that pressed against her.

"Why?" She forced out the word, her voice breathless.

He drew back, as if he'd just realized how close he was. "Maybe it would be better if I took the lead in talking to them. If they don't already know that Tony was married—"

"Yes, of course you're right." That was yet another nightmare to think about. Tony's family would have no reason to welcome, or believe in, a previously unknown wife. "Just—"

"What?"

She hesitated a moment and then shook her head. "I was going to say be tactful, but maybe there's nothing left to be tactful about."

He squeezed her hand, so lightly that she might have imagined it. "I'll do my best."

She slid out of the car and waited until he joined her on the sidewalk. The gate shrieked in protest when he pushed it open, and she followed him up the walk, stepping over the cracks where weeds flourished unchecked.

Three steps up to a concrete stoop, and then Zach rapped sharply on the door, ignoring the doorbell. Moments passed. The lace curtain on the window beside the door twitched. Someone was checking them out.

They must have looked presentable, because the woman swung the door open. "Something I can do for you?"

She was probably not more than thirty, Caro guessed. Blond hair, dark roots showing, was pulled back into a ponytail. She wore a faded navy cardigan over a waitress uniform, and the bag slung over her shoulder seemed to say that she had either just come in or was just going out.

"We're looking for Anthony Gibson. Does he live here?"

She jerked a nod and turned to look over her shoulder. "Somebody for you, Tony. Listen, I have to go. I'll see you later."

She held the door so that they could enter and then slid past them as if eager to make her departure.

"What do you folks want?" The tone held a trace of suspicion. The man thumped his way toward them with a walker. Tall, like Tony, with dark eyes.

But the world was full of tall men with dark eyes. Surely this couldn't be Tony's father. The setting was wrong, and he must be too old—he looked nearly as old as Grams, rather than being a contemporary of her mother.

"You're Tony Gibson?" Zach nudged her forward as he spoke.

"That's right." The man came to a stop at a mustard-colored recliner and sat, shoving the walker to one side.

"I'm Zachary Burkhalter, Chief of Police over in

Churchville in Lancaster County. This is Caroline Hampton. We wanted to talk to you about your son."

She opened her mouth to say that this couldn't be her Tony's father, and then she closed it again, because Tony's picture sat on top of the upright piano in the corner. A much younger Tony, but that smile was unmistakable.

The lines in the man's face seemed to grow deeper. "My son died a month ago. If he owed you money, you're wasting your time coming here for it."

"No, nothing like that," Zach said easily. "We're just trying to clear up some questions that came up after Tony's death. We weren't sure we had the right family."

The old man—Tony's father, she reminded herself— leaned back in the recliner, grabbing the handle so that the footrest flipped up. "My son, all right." He pointed to the picture on the piano. "If that's the Tony Gibson you're looking for."

"Yes." She forced herself to speak. "Yes, it is."

"Died out west. New Mexico, it was." He didn't look grieved, just resigned. "I always figured it would happen that way. Somebody'd call and tell us he was gone."

"What made you think that?" Zach's voice had gentled, as if he recognized pain behind the resignation.

He shrugged. "Always skating too near the edge of the law, Tony was. You can't keep doing that and not get into trouble at some point."

"Had you heard from him lately?" *Did he tell you about me?* That was what she wanted to ask, but something held her back.

"Not for months. He sent Mary Alice a hundred bucks back in January, I think it was. Said she should get Christmas presents with it."

Mary Alice was apparently the woman who'd opened the door to them. Tony's sister, she supposed, left here to look after their ailing father.

"Were you expecting a visit from him this spring?" She put the question abruptly, hearing Tony's voice in her mind. *We'll go back east in the spring, sweetheart. We'll surprise both our families.* He'd spun her around in a hug. *My folks will be crazy about you.*

"No. And I wouldn't have believed him if he had said so." He planted his hands on the arms of the recliner and leaned toward her. "What is all this, anyway? Why do you want to know about my son? What are you to him?"

"We just—" Zach began, but she shook her head.

"Don't, Zach." She took a breath. For good or ill, the man had a right to know she was his son's widow. "I'm sorry to blurt it out this way, Mr. Gibson. I'm actually Caroline Hampton Gibson. I was married to Tony."

He didn't speak, but a wave of red flushed alarmingly into his face. He jerked the recliner back into the upright position with a thump.

She took a step backward. "I don't want anything from you. I just thought you ought to know—"

"You're crazy, that's what you are." He grabbed the walker and took a step toward her. "Or you're trying to pull something. Some of his friends, most likely, just as crooked as he was."

"Nothing like that." Zach's tone was soothing.

The old man ignored him, glaring at Caroline. "I don't know who you are. But I know who you're not. You're not my son's wife. Mary Alice is Tony's wife, and she's the mother of his little girl."

NINE

Caroline spread the old quilt over the table in the barn, handling it as carefully as if it were a living creature. Maybe working on the quilt would distract her from the memory of yesterday's shocking revelations.

Maybe, but she doubted it.

She forced herself to concentrate on the pattern. The research she'd done had told her that the particular way the flying geese and star were combined on this quilt was unusual. She wanted to see it more clearly, but the colors were muted by an inevitable coating of dust. Going over it with the brush attachment of the vacuum cleaner on low power was the recommended process.

The soft hum of the vacuum blocked out other sounds. Unfortunately, it couldn't block out her thoughts. They kept leaping rebelliously back to that disastrous trip to Philadelphia.

Maybe *disastrous* wasn't the right word. The revelations, one after the other, had been painful, but would she be better off if she didn't know? The truth would be the truth, whether she wanted to hear it or not.

She still wasn't sure how she'd gotten out of that house after Tony's father had dropped his bombshell.

Zach had taken over, of course. That would always be his automatic response. He'd soothed the man as best he could and piloted her back to the car.

She hadn't been able to talk about it during the drive back. Maybe it would have been better to get it out, but she couldn't. She'd been numb, maybe in shock.

Zach hadn't pressed her, other than to urge her to tell her grandmother or her sisters what happened. He'd left her with the promise that he'd check the records and find out the facts.

She hadn't taken Zach's advice, good as it probably was. She'd been in limbo, unable to decide anything. She'd spent the evening with Grams and Rachel, taking comfort in their chatter, listening to Grams's stories, reviving a sense of belonging she hadn't had in a very long time.

She switched off the vacuum and stood back to look at the results. The experts appeared to be right—the area she'd gone over was discernibly brighter, the deep, saturated colors coming to life.

The sound of a step had her turning, seeing the shadow he cast in the patch of sunlight on the barn boards before she saw him. Zach stood in the doorway, his figure a dark shape against the brightness outside.

His uniform didn't induce that instinctive revulsion any longer, but her stomach still tightened at the sight of him. He might have found out. He might know the truth about her marriage.

"Hi. Your sister told me I'd find you here." He came toward her, heels sounding on the wide planks. A shaft of sunlight turned his sandy hair to gold for a moment, and then it darkened when he moved out of the light. He studied the quilt. "Are you taking up quilting now?"

"This is the quilt your sister and I were talking about. It apparently dates from the 1850s. I'm trying, very cautiously, to clean it up." She was a coward, but she'd rather talk about the quilt than what had brought him here.

"I'm surprised Agatha Morris wasn't interested. I'd expect her to be here leaning over your shoulder, telling you you're doing it all wrong."

"I may be, but eight out of ten experts on the Internet agreed that vacuuming with a soft brush was a good first step."

"What would we do without the Internet?"

He said the words casually, but she heard something beneath them that alerted her.

"You've found out, haven't you?" She let go of the vacuum hose, and it clattered to the floor.

He nodded toward a bench against the low wall that separated the hay mow from the rest of the barn floor. "Let's have a seat. I see Cal left behind some of the improvements he made when this was his workshop."

She followed him, not interested in whether her brother-in-law had made the bench or not, just intent on sitting down before her knees did something stupid.

"The Internet does make searching records easier. Tony married Mary Alice seven years ago in Philadelphia."

She ought to be shaken, shocked and appalled. Maybe she was, but at the moment she mostly seemed numb. "You're sure—" She shook her head. "Of course you're sure, or you wouldn't be telling me. What about the child?"

"Their daughter, Allison Mary, was born seven months later. A shotgun wedding, maybe."

It would be tempting to try and rationalize what Tony had done in that light, but she found she couldn't. He'd had a wife. A child. He had a duty to them, not to her.

"Did he get a divorce?" A voice she barely recognized as hers asked the question.

He hesitated for a moment, as if knowing how much this would hurt her. His very silence told her the answer before he said the word.

"No." His stretched his arm along the back of the bench and touched her shoulder. "I'm sorry, Caroline."

She nodded, trying to think this through. "So the marriage he went through with me wasn't legal. Am I— did I do anything against the law in marrying him?"

"No. He was the bigamist, not you."

She took a deep breath. "I guess mostly I don't understand. He must have known I'd find out the truth eventually. Why would he do such a thing?"

"That's a good question. Can you think of any reason—anything that might explain what was going through his mind?"

"If I could, don't you think I'd have mentioned that by now? There's nothing." She planted her hands on her knees. "Maybe if I threw something I'd feel better— preferably something at Tony's head."

"I don't think that would help." His voice was mild, as it always was. That didn't tell her whether he believed her or not. "It's natural enough to be angry at him."

"He's well beyond the reach of my anger now." That in itself was cause for wrath. Tony had escaped, and left her to deal with everything. "I'm relieved about one thing, though. Since I wasn't really his wife, I don't have to do anything about that money."

He didn't answer. Didn't move. How, then, did she know that he wanted something—something in relation to the money?

"What?" Impatience threaded her voice.

"You should talk to the Santa Fe police about it. They're the ones investigating his death, and it could have an impact upon that case."

"I don't want to." Her fingers twisted together in her lap. He put his hand over hers, stilling the restless movement.

"That's pretty obvious. Would you mind telling me why?"

Zach studied the expression on Caroline's face. What was going on with her? For that matter, what was going on with him? He ought to be looking at this situation, at her, with his usual professional detachment.

He wasn't managing to do that, not where Caroline was concerned. She got under his skin in a way he'd never experienced before.

She wasn't his type. Take that as a starting point. Sure, he was attracted to her. Any man would be. But this was about more than creamy skin and eyes so deep a green that a man could drown in them.

He was drawn by what he sensed beneath that—the creativity that sparked and sizzled in her, the gentle smile that didn't come often enough, the hint of vulnerability mixed with strength and independence.

His arguments seemed to be heading him in the wrong direction. Against that, he stacked who he was. A cop. A family man. A father who wouldn't bring a woman into his daughter's life unless he was sure she was the right woman. A Christian woman.

He must have been silent too long, because Caroline turned her head to look at him.

"Aren't you going to argue with me?"

"I guess I should." He didn't want to. He sympathized with her, maybe too much. She'd been through a tragedy that would be tough for anyone to handle, especially someone who didn't have a relationship with Christ to see her through.

He looked up at the lofty barn roof, where dust motes danced in the stripes of sunlight. Something about the quiet, open space made him feel as if he was in church.

Lord, show me how to deal with this. Caroline is hurting. I want to help her, but I have to do my duty.

"I don't see why I should do the police's work for them." Caroline's tone was defensive, and she sent him a sidelong glance that was reminiscent of Ruthie when she was in a stubborn mood. "I haven't done anything wrong, and even if Tony did, surely his liability died with him."

He studied her averted face. "Is Tony dead?"

Her gaze flashed to him. "Yes. The police said he was. I buried him."

"So the things that have happened since you came here—the letter, the coffee, the safe-deposit box—were they coincidences? Someone trying to make you think Tony is still alive?"

Her lips trembled for a moment, and she pressed them firmly together. She shook her head. "I don't know. Nothing else has happened. Maybe nothing will. Maybe—"

"Do you really think that?" He was sorry for her, but he couldn't let her convince herself that she could just walk away from this.

She shoved her hair back from her face in that characteristic gesture. "I'd like to, but I guess I can't. Still, according to you I'm not Tony's wife. So why should I be involved?"

He couldn't tell her that Tony had been under investigation by the Santa Fe police—that was their business, and he couldn't interfere unless they asked for his help. But she already suspected gambling, didn't she?

"If Tony was involved in something that skirted the law, as his father said, that money could be important. The police should know."

"Why should I be the one to tell them? It properly belongs to Mary Alice, doesn't it? Let her tell them."

"She doesn't know about it. Come on, Caroline, stop evading the issue. Why won't you go to the police?"

She swung to face him, anger flaring in her eyes. "You know the answer to that, don't you? I don't know what happens to other people who've been where I was, but I know what effect it had on me. I've spent the past eight years being so law abiding it's painful—obeying every last little rule and regulation, never jay-walking, never so much as getting a parking ticket."

"Because you learned respect for the law." He was feeling his way, not sure what lay behind that vehemence.

"No! Because I can never put myself in that helpless position again. Because I learned I couldn't trust anyone—not my family and not the police."

She swung away from him, breathing hard, as if sorry she'd revealed that much of herself to him. He couldn't let her stop, not when she was so close to letting him see what was going on inside her.

"What happened? Tell me. You got into trouble, but there's more to it than that."

She shook her head, mouth set, eyes shimmering with tears that she no doubt didn't want him to see.

"You were riding around with two guys," he said deliberately. "You stayed outside in the car as a lookout while they went into a convenience store and beat up the elderly proprietor."

"No." The word seemed torn from her. "I didn't. I didn't know what they were doing. I had no idea they were robbing that man." Her voice trembled, the pain in it almost convincing him.

"Did your lawyer bring that up at the trial?"

"My lawyer didn't believe anything I told him." A touch of bitterness. "Or maybe he didn't care."

"Your family could have gotten different representation for you." They hadn't; he knew that. Why not?

For a moment she stared, eyes wide and clouded, as if she looked into the past. "The authorities couldn't find my mother. Turned out she'd run off to Palm Springs with her latest boyfriend. You couldn't expect her to pass up a trip like that just because her kid was in trouble, could you?"

The insight into what her life had been like with her mother shook him. He'd heard bits and pieces from time to time about Lily Hampton, none of it good.

"Your grandparents, your sisters—"

She shook her head. "I guess they tried to help, when they finally heard, but by then I was in the system. There wasn't much they could do. Besides, my mother was my legal guardian." Her voice shook a little. She might deny it, but that youthful betrayal had affected the rest of her life.

He understood, only too well. Once a juvenile was in the system, everything affecting them had to grind through the legal process. "Your grandmother must have been frantic."

"I suppose." Doubt touched her eyes. "At the time, all I could see was that they'd let me down."

"You got through it." He couldn't imagine how much strength it must have taken for her to deal with that situation alone at her age.

"Not without scars."

Lord, help me to understand. "That's not all, is it?" He knew, without questioning how, that there had been more. That something worse had happened to her when she was alone and vulnerable. "Locked up in a place like that—the other kids must have—"

"Not the other kids." Her body tensed, as if she drew into herself. "I dealt with them."

"Who?" He had to force the word out, because he thought he knew the answer, and he didn't want to hear it.

She hugged herself, as if cold in spite of the warmth of the day. "I don't want—"

"Who was it?" His voice was sharp to his ears. "A cop?"

She pressed her lips together. Nodded. "When I was arrested." It came out in a whisper. "He took me into a room by myself at the police station. Left me there. I thought my mother would come, but she didn't. He came back. He—" Her breath caught, as if she choked on the word.

"He attacked you." He managed, somehow, through the red haze of fury that nearly choked him, to keep the words gentle.

The muscles in her neck worked. She nodded. "Someone came in, finally. He said I was faking, trying to get him in trouble. I didn't care what he said, as long as I didn't have to see him again."

She should have filed a complaint, but he could understand why she hadn't. She'd been alone, and she'd just had a harsh lesson in how helpless she was. Small wonder she didn't trust the system or anyone involved in it.

If he'd been the one to walk into that room, he'd have been tempted to dispense some harsh justice of his own to the man who'd abused his position and shamed his badge. Even now he wanted to put his fist through the barn wall.

But that wouldn't help Caroline. He was probably the last person who could help her, but he was the one she'd confided in, and he had to try.

"He was a criminal wearing a badge, and I'd like to see him get the justice that's due him. But he was only one person. You had the misfortune to have run up against him."

To say nothing of the poor excuse for a mother she'd had. Seemed as if Caroline had been given the raw end of the deal too many times.

"I know." She straightened, quickly blotting a tear that had escaped as if ashamed of it. "Intellectually, I know that. But that doesn't keep me from wanting to stay as far away from the police as I possibly can."

"Understandable." It was a good thing she'd pulled herself together, because he longed to put his arm around her, pull her close, tell her—

No. There was nothing he could tell her. He might understand her better now, but that understanding had only served to emphasize the barrier between them.

She pushed herself off the bench, taking a few quick steps away from him. Maybe she sensed the feelings he was trying so hard to suppress.

"Look—about the money. You could tell the Santa Fe police about it, couldn't you? Tell them it isn't mine. That I don't want anything to do with it."

"I can tell them." That wouldn't end her involvement, but he didn't have the heart to tell her that now. Push her too hard, and Caroline might just run again.

He could understand why she always seemed to perch on the edge of flight. Nothing in her life had given her the assurance that she could trust people, and running away had been her only defense.

"It'll be okay." He stood, went to her. Wanted to touch her, but he didn't quite dare, knowing what he did. "You're not a helpless kid any longer, and you have family to love and protect you."

She had him to protect her, too, even though she probably didn't believe that and wouldn't welcome it. Still, he was the one she'd told. That had to mean something.

"Since you haven't called me again, I realized the only way I'd find out how you're doing is to call you." Francine's voice was clear and crisp over the cell phone. Possibly a little annoyed, as well.

"I'm sorry." Caroline curled into the corner of the leather sofa. She'd closed the curtains against the darkness outside and told herself she was perfectly safe. Still, it was good to hear another person's voice. "It's been so hectic here, getting settled and trying to get into the craft-show circuit. That's no excuse. I should have called."

"Craft shows?" The words were dismissive. "Really, Caroline. You have a position waiting for you here. I've told you that. Why don't you come back to Santa Fe where you belong?"

"I'm not sure I do belong there." Odd, how far away that life seemed now. "Maybe what happened with Tony changed everything."

"Nonsense. You had a good life here before you ever met Tony, didn't you? There's no reason why you can't have that again."

"I'll think about it." That was an evasion, but how could she know what she wanted? She'd been battered by one shock after another until it was impossible to do anything except tense up, waiting for the next one. "What's going on with the gallery? Are you all right?"

"Never mind me. How are you?" Francine's voice softened on the words. Caro could picture her, leaning back in her custom-made desk chair, her sleek blond hair shining under the indirect lighting she insisted upon. "I didn't mean to snap, but I've been worried about you. So many people have asked how you are, and I don't know what to tell them."

"I'm fine. Really." It was good to feel she had friends who cared about her. "It's just—things have been a little crazy." She could trust Francine, but it didn't seem fair to unload all her worries on her.

"You're not. I can hear it in your voice. What is it? Have you heard from Tony?"

The question had her sitting bolt upright. "Why would you ask that? Tony's dead."

Francine didn't speak for a moment, but her very silence communicated her doubt. "I know that's what the police said. What we all believed. But after you told me about the man who accosted you that day—"

"You've found out something." She was shaken, but at some level she wasn't surprised. Francine knew everyone who was anyone in Santa Fe, and she heard every rumor first.

"Nothing that I'd want to take to the police." Francine sounded unsure of herself, and that was unusual. "People have been talking. People liked Tony. He was good at selling upscale real estate, probably because he was so likeable. But now there are rumors of gambling debts—enough rumors that there must be some basis in fact, I'd think. You had no idea?"

"No." It was hard to look back and see how naive she'd been. "But now—" She didn't want to tell Francine about the safe-deposit box stuffed with money, but if that didn't indicate gambling, what else could it have been?

"Now it seems likely to you. Don't bother to deny it. I can hear it in your voice." Francine had become her usual brisk self. "Well, that increases the possibility that Tony is still alive. And if so, he'll get in touch with you. You're his wife, and he—"

"I'm not." She couldn't let Francine go on any longer making assumptions that weren't true about her relationship with Tony. "I found out yesterday Tony had a wife in Philadelphia. He didn't bother to divorce her before he married me."

"I can't believe it. Caroline, are you sure? He must have been divorced. He couldn't hope to get away with anything else."

"But he did, didn't he? I had no idea the woman

existed, any more than she knew about me." Her throat tightened, and she had to force the words out. "He had a child with her."

"Oh, my dear. I'm so sorry."

Somehow the sympathy in Francine's voice broke through the control Caroline had imposed on her emotions. A sob burst out before she could stop it, then another. She could only hold the phone like a lifeline and let the tears spill out, vaguely registering the soothing words Francine uttered.

Finally she managed to take a deep breath, mopping her face with her palm. "Sorry." Her voice was still choked. "I didn't mean to let go that way."

"Well, it's not surprising. But look, are you positive about this? How did you find out? Did your family help you, hire a private investigator?"

"No, nothing like that. I haven't told them about it yet. The local police chief got involved. He's the one who found the record of Tony's marriage, and no record of any divorce."

"A country cop?" That was Francine at her most superior. "My dear, if you're depending on someone like that, you're really in trouble. It sounds as if what you need right now is a friend you can count on."

She pressed her palm over her burning eyes. "I know how lucky I am to have you."

"Well, I'm not much use to you when I'm way out here. Let's see—" she could hear the tapping of computer keys "—there are a few things on my calendar I can't rearrange, but I ought to be free in a couple of days. I'll let you know when my flight gets in."

Her mind grappled to keep up. "You're coming here?"

"Why not? I suppose that inn of yours can rent me a room, can't it?"

"But I can't let you do that. You have so much to do. The gallery—"

"I own the gallery, remember? I can give myself a vacation whenever I want to."

"Francine, I appreciate it." Her voice choked again. "I can't tell you how much. But I can't let you change your plans for me."

"There's no point in arguing about it. I'm sure you think you can handle things by yourself, but right now it sounds as if you can use a friend."

She'd make another attempt to dissuade her, but Francine was right. She did need a friend, and it was far better to rely on someone she'd known for over two years than someone she'd known for less than two weeks.

An image of Zach's frowning face formed in her mind. What did she know about him, really? And what had made her trust him with secrets she hadn't told another soul?

TEN

Caroline folded the tortilla over the chicken-and-pepper-jack-cheese filling. She'd come over to the house to show Grams how the quilt looked after its initial cleaning, and ended up offering to cook supper. She just hoped they'd like her chicken enchiladas. There weren't too many recipes in her repertoire. She'd had to make some substitutions, since Snyder's Grocery apparently considered that one kind of pepper was sufficient for anyone's needs.

Grams came into the kitchen, carrying a large document box—that sort that was used to store fragile paper and photographs. "Here it is. I'm sure you'll find something in this batch of papers and letters about the quilt."

Caro gestured with the tortilla she'd just warmed in the microwave. "Great. I don't dare touch them now, but I'll look through them after supper."

Grams found nothing unusual about her interest in the quilt, attributing it to a natural desire to learn about her family history. Caro didn't think it was that, exactly, but she couldn't explain, even to herself, the fascination the old quilt held for her.

"There's no hurry. You can take the box back to the apartment with you."

Grams turned to set it on the end of the counter, her earrings swinging. Caro couldn't help a smile. Grams wore the earrings she'd made for her almost every day.

"I'll be careful with it," she promised.

"I know you will, dear. And after all, family documents belong to you as much as anyone."

That calm assumption that she had a place here still took her aback, even though she'd already encountered it several times. To Grams, it was as if Caroline's time away was just a visit to another world, and now she was back where she belonged.

"Your grandfather started collecting family papers and letters after he retired, with some idea of writing a family history." Grams's smile was reminiscent. "He should have known he wouldn't be content with something that sedentary. He loved to be out and about, meeting with his friends and taking an interest in civic affairs."

"I wish I had more memories of him." She'd been too young when Mom took them away, and time had blurred whatever memories had been left.

Grams came to hug her, her cheek soft against Caro's. "He loved you, you know. You'd sit on his lap and listen to his stories until you fell asleep in his arms."

Her throat tightened. "Thank you, Grams." For the memory, and for the sense of belonging. She wiped away a tear. "And thanks again for being so welcoming about Francine coming."

"Well, of course it's fine for your friend to come. She can have the blue bedroom. We don't have any guests booked until the weekend." Grams pulled the wooden stool over so that she could watch the enchilada-making. "Goodness, Caro, wouldn't you know we'd welcome your friend?"

"I know nothing hampers your hospitality. I just thought it might be an imposition if you have other guests booked. Although I'm sure Francine will insist on paying."

"She'll do no such thing." Grams's response was prompt. "She's your friend."

Grams and Francine could battle that one out, she decided. They were both so strong-willed that she didn't have a clue which one would win.

She transferred the enchiladas to one of Rachel's ceramic baking pans, trying to concentrate on that instead of on the vague worry that had possessed her since hearing of Francine's plans.

The thing that bothered her about the proposed visit didn't have anything to do with Grams's hospitality. It was more of a reluctance to see two such different parts of her life meeting. The truth was that she felt like a different person since she'd come back to Pennsylvania. With Francine here, who would she be?

She didn't think she wanted to go back to who she'd been in Santa Fe—the woman who'd fallen in love with Tony and who'd also fallen for his lies. But she wasn't sure she was ready to move forward, either.

"Are you all right, dear?" Grams touched her arm, her fingertips light as the wings of a butterfly. "You know I've been worrying about you. And praying for you, of course."

Her throat tightened. "I know. I'm going to be all right."

"Grieving takes time," Grams said, her voice gentle. "You can't rush it."

Shame flooded her. She couldn't keep doing this—couldn't go on letting Grams imagine she was grieving for a beloved husband. She set the casserole dish in the oven, closed the door and turned to face her grandmother.

"It's not what you think. The situation with Tony—" She stopped, because Rachel walked into the kitchen, the dog at her heels.

Rachel glanced from one to the other of them, obviously knowing she'd interrupted something. "Should I make some excuse none of us will believe and go away?"

"No. Don't go. I want both of you to hear this." They deserved to hear the truth. Caro took a breath, trying to frame the words she needed to speak. "I fell in love with Tony at first sight, I guess, enough in love to agree when he wanted to elope. But I didn't know him very well." That was a massive understatement.

Rachel came to lean on the table, as if wanting to be closer to her. "You found out you made a mistake."

"That's a nice way of putting it." She tried to smile, but she couldn't manage it. "It didn't take long to find out that Tony lied constantly—about where he'd been, about his business dealings. He wiped out my savings and checking accounts. When I confronted him—" They didn't need to know about all the hurtful words Tony had thrown at her. "He was furious. He left, and that was the night he died."

"Oh, honey—"

She held out her hand, stopping Rachel's instinctive embrace. There was more to be said before she could let herself accept comfort. "I never did find out what he was doing, but I think he might have been involved in gambling. The other day, when I went to

Philadelphia…" She couldn't watch their reactions. "I learned he was married before. Apparently he never got a divorce. So it looks as if our wedding wasn't even legal."

Silence for a moment. And then she felt Rachel's arms go around her, strong and comforting, the way she had been when Caroline was eight and had broken her arm falling out of a tree. "Caro, I'm so sorry."

She nodded, those weak tears spilling over again. Grams's arms went around both of them, holding them tight.

"You cry all you want, Caro. You don't have to be brave for us."

Maybe that was what she needed to hear to give her strength. "I'm all right." She pressed her cheek against Grams's, and then hugged her sister. "I've cried enough over it. I just wanted you to understand that—" She stopped, not sure what she wanted to say.

"That some odd things have been happening since you got back," Rachel finished for her.

Caroline drew back, shock running through her. "How did you know that? Did Zach tell you?"

"No, he didn't say a word, but I'm not an idiot. I can see what's right in front of me. If he's helping you…well, he's a good man."

"We want to help you," Grams said. "But we don't want you to think we're interfering." Grams brushed her hair back from her face with a gentle touch. "We're on your side, that's all. We love you. Just remember that."

She nodded, wiping tears away, and gave a watery laugh. "I'll remember. I love you, too."

She'd told them the worst of it. No one had blamed

her or looked at her with that pitying expression that she dreaded. Only with love.

Caroline came down the stairs from the loft, still yawning, and squinted at the bright sunlight flooding through the living room windows. She crossed to the sofa, mindful of the papers she'd left spread across it and the coffee table.

She'd sat up far later than she'd intended, absorbed in the contents of the box Grams had given her. Those fragile papers, with their faded ink, shouldn't be left where sunlight might touch them. She didn't know much about preserving old documents, but common sense told her that.

Still, her fingers lingered as she started sorting them back into the box. Grandfather hadn't, as far as she could tell, done anything more than put together whatever he'd found relating to the 1850s and '60s. The papers weren't grouped in any way, and she'd found the Civil War enlistment papers of one Christian Unger shoved in among a sheaf of household bills and letters.

The letters were what fascinated her. Most of the ones she'd found so far dated from the 1850s. Elizabeth Chapman Unger, Grandfather's grandmother and the maker of her quilt, had come from Boston, Massachusetts. She seemed to have kept up a lively correspondence with her sister, Abigail, after she married and moved to Churchville. Judging by Abigail's replies, Elizabeth had found plenty to say about her new surroundings and her husband's family, apparently not all of it complimentary.

Caro smiled at one passage, where Abigail urged her

sister to be tactful with her new mother-in-law. Human nature hadn't changed very much in the past 150 years.

She laid the papers gently back into the box and put the lid on. There'd been no mention of the quilt in what she'd found so far. Maybe the best thing would be to sort out everything she could find that related to Elizabeth and then go through it chronologically. Grams had promised to continue looking for anything else that related to her. The old house held the accumulated belongings of at least ten generations of the Unger family, and finding any one thing could be a challenge.

Grams had also suggested that Emma Zook would be a good person to give advice about repairing the quilt. She had a long tradition of quilting, as most Amish women did, and she'd know how to handle it.

But that could come later. Right now she was starving, and Rachel had insisted she come to the house for breakfast this morning to taste a new frittata recipe. Over supper last night, as if by unspoken consent, they'd kept the conversation on quilts and food, not on Caro's painful revelations.

She slid the box into the closet and headed out the door, careful to lock it behind her. Nothing had happened recently, but still, she didn't intend to take any chances.

She paused, hand still on the knob, wondering at the turn of phrase. Chances of what? Was she afraid that someone was trying to convince her that Tony was still alive? Or afraid that he was?

Tony wasn't her husband. At some point over the past two days she'd accepted that. She didn't have any obligation to him.

But she'd made the promises before God. She'd

meant them, even if Tony had been lying the whole time. Her mind winced away from the memory of that ceremony. Tony, so tall and handsome in the dark suit he'd worn, seeming so solemn when he took his vows.

Had he been laughing inside, even then? She didn't know, and the more she thought about it, the less sure she became that she could rely on anything she thought she knew about him.

Well, standing here obsessing about it wasn't going to help. She started down the path that led around the corner of the barn. She was far better off to get on with things. She'd have breakfast, see if there was anything helpful she could do at the inn this morning.

This afternoon she'd work on the quilt and try to get a few more things ready for the next craft show. Once the moving company got around to bringing the rest of her belongings, she'd have a better choice of things to sell. There was an entire box of jewelry and some weaving that she'd left for the movers.

She ought to be working on jewelry instead of the quilt. Some simple pendants that she could price at under twenty dollars would be a good balance to the more expensive pieces. Plenty of people went looking for bargains, or what they thought were bargains, anyway, at craft shows.

The path led around the pond, past the gazebo toward the house. She glanced back at the barn and stopped. One of the double doors into the barn stood ajar a couple of inches.

Had she left it that way after that disturbing talk with Zach yesterday? Surely not. She was careful to lock things up, although there wasn't much in the barn to attract a thief—just the quilt frame she'd set up and the table on which she'd laid the quilt to vacuum it. She'd packed the quilt up afterward to take to the Zook farm.

Coffee and frittata were waiting at the house. She sighed. It would worry her all through breakfast if she didn't check now, just to be sure.

She cut across the lawn toward the barn doors, the damp grass soaking her sneakers in only a few steps. Well, that was foolish. She should have backtracked along the walk instead of trying to save time.

She went up the gravel ramp to the upper level of the barn, slowing as she reached the door. Silly, to be worried about it. She'd probably left it that way herself. Certainly she'd been cut up enough emotionally after betraying herself to Zach. Hardly surprising if she'd forgotten a little something like shutting the barn door.

But at some level she knew it wasn't true. She'd closed the door and made sure it was latched, just as she always did.

She reached out, grasping the handle. Everything was perfectly still, except for the family of barn swallows who chirped under the eaves. If someone had been there, he or she wouldn't hang around to be found. She shoved the door open and took a step inside.

Sunlight poured through the opening, casting a spotlight on the interior. Nearly empty, just as she'd left it.

Except that the table she'd been working on had been tipped over, and the quilting frame she'd brought down from the loft had been smashed to pieces.

Zach sat at the kitchen table at the inn, steam rising from the coffee mug Rachel had just set in front of him. By the looks of her, Caroline was the one who needed the coffee, but instead she was holding a cup of chamomile tea that her grandmother had forced on her.

Mrs. Unger and Rachel were hovering over Caroline, so he waited, letting them do all the fussing they needed to before he started in with more questions.

Come to think of it, their concern seemed a bit out of proportion to the cause. If so, that probably meant Caroline had finally told them about her husband. High time, too. They were capable of dealing with that trouble.

He'd sat in this kitchen before. The Hampton women seemed to be—well, not trouble in themselves, exactly. It was more as if they found trouble.

Or in Caroline's case, brought it with her. He took a sip of the coffee, nearly scalding his tongue. Everything that had happened since she arrived had its roots in her life in Santa Fe—that seemed certain.

"You ought to have some breakfast." Rachel gestured toward a casserole that sat on top of the stove, still bubbling from its time in the oven. "I'm sure we called you out before you had time to eat."

"No, thanks. I had breakfast with Ruthie before she left for school. Now, about the damage—"

"It's just a good thing Caro left the quilt in the house last night," Mrs. Unger said. "I'd hate to think what they might have done to it."

So she was assuming the unknown intruders were vandals. Most likely that was true, but he didn't want to take anything for granted.

"This quilt—was it the one I saw you working on yesterday?"

Caroline nodded. Her face was a little pale. Natural enough, having vandalism strike so close to her.

She'd been getting the dust off it with a vacuum brush when he'd come in, he remembered. "Is it valuable?"

She looked up, seeming startled. "I don't know. We hadn't really looked into the value of it."

"I gave the quilt to Caro because she loved it," Mrs. Unger said. "No one is thinking about selling it, so its value is immaterial."

"Not to someone who planned on stealing it," he pointed out.

"Surely this wasn't intended to be a theft." Rachel poured a little more coffee in his cup, even though he hadn't taken much more than a sip. "If someone wanted to steal an antique quilt, they'd hit a quilt shop. There are several between here and Lancaster."

"I suppose, but I can't ignore the possibility. The more valuable the quilt, the more likely, it seems to me."

"I suppose we could find out." Caroline threaded her fingers back through her hair, letting it ruffle down to the shoulder of the white shirt she wore with jeans. That was probably the most conservative outfit he'd seen her wear yet. "I described the quilt to Agatha Morris, though, and she seemed to disregard it."

"Agatha doesn't know everything." Mrs. Unger's voice was tart. "We could call an expert for a valuation, if you think it's important."

"That wouldn't be a bad idea." It also wouldn't be a bad idea if he could speak to Caroline alone, but that didn't seem likely, the way her grandmother and sister were protecting her.

"I'm not worried about what it's worth. There's just

something about the quilt that speaks to me." Caroline gave him an assessing look. Can you understand that? That was what it seemed to say.

"Right." He pulled a notebook from his pocket and put it on the table next to his mug. He didn't need to write any of this down, but somehow people seemed to find the action reassuring. "Now, who might know about the quilt?"

She frowned down at the straw-colored brew. "I talked about it at the quilt show, I know. To your sister. She was the one who suggested I speak to Mrs. Morris." She shrugged. "There were a lot of people milling around. I suppose anyone might have heard us. But if someone did want to steal the quilt, why smash up the quilting frame?"

"Good point. It's most likely vandals. Something about spring seems to bring them out of the woodwork. I don't suppose any of you have seen anyone hanging around the place?"

Blank looks, heads shaken. People didn't notice, unless they were the type who saw lurkers in every innocent bystander.

"Maybe you should move into the house." Mrs. Unger's brow wrinkled as she looked at her youngest granddaughter. "If you had run into them, whoever they were—"

Caroline patted her grandmother's hand. "I didn't, and I hope I'm smart enough not to go wandering around investigating strange noises by myself."

"Did you hear any noises?" He slid the question in. She should have—that was the first thing that struck him. The damage had to have made considerable noise, and her apartment was on the other side of the barn wall.

She was already shaking her head. "No. I've been

thinking about that, and I should have if they were in there at night. But I spent the evening in the house, and we wouldn't have heard anything from here."

"That explains it, then." He supposed. It got dark fairly early, so the damage could have been done any time after, say, seven in the evening. Still, whoever had done it was taking a chance on being seen.

He wasn't accusing her of lying to him, not even in his mind. But no matter how sympathetic he felt toward Caroline, he couldn't let that affect his judgment.

He put the notebook in his pocket as he stood. "Well, I think that's it for now." He looked at Caroline. "If you'd like to walk out with me, maybe we could have a word about the locks."

She nodded, getting up quickly. "I'll be back in a minute," she said, and followed him to the door.

The patio was sun drenched and bright with spring flowers. Caroline stopped at the low wall that surrounded it and looked at him.

"This isn't about locks, is it?"

"No, I guess not, although it wouldn't hurt to put dead bolts on all the doors. More to the point, why don't you want to move into the house? Seems like that would be the sensible thing to do."

She shrugged, evading his eyes. "No one has ever described me as sensible."

"Your grandmother would probably feel better."

"You mean she'd be able to fuss over me more." She folded her arms across her chest.

"That's not a bad thing, you know." He could understand why she was prickly, given her history, but her grandmother obviously loved her.

"I like my independence." Her mouth set in a stubborn line.

He looked at her for a long moment, weighing how much to say. "I hope that's it," he said slowly. "I hope you're not just staying there because you want to make it easier for Tony to reach you."

He thought she'd flare up at hearing her words parroted back at her. She didn't. She just looked at him, her gaze defiant, and he knew that was exactly why she was so determined to stay.

ELEVEN

"That is just right." Emma Zook smiled at Caro over the quilt that was spread out between them. "You already know how to take the tiny stitches so they will not show."

"I've never done anything like this before." She traced the line of stitches she'd used to repair the fraying edge of a triangle. As Emma said, it was nearly invisible.

Nancy, Emma's daughter-in-law, came to look over her shoulder at the quilt. "That will fix up nice, it will. It is good to keep such a quilt in the family."

"Yes, it is."

Funny. For years she'd told herself she got by very nicely without family. Her priorities seemed to have gotten turned around in recent months.

Nancy smoothed a strand of hair back under the white prayer cap that sat on the back of her head. "Sticky buns are almost ready to come out of the oven. We'll have some with coffee when you finish work."

She'd decline on the basis that a sticky bun contained probably her entire daily allotment of calories, but that would no doubt be an offense against hospitality. Nancy fed her family in the way that Amish women had done for generations, and they seemed to thrive on it. Of course, they had no need for organized activities or gym memberships to keep fit. Dealing with the daily needs of the house and farm without electricity or other modern conveniences did the job.

Emma fingered the binding on the edges of the quilt, frowning a little. "The binding shows wear first. Could be you should just put on a new one."

"I'd hate to replace it with modern fabric. From everything I've heard, that takes away from the value. Maybe I can repair it."

Emma nodded. "It is worth a try. You have the patience to do it right. Like with the jewelry you make."

Emma didn't wear jewelry, of course, but that didn't seem to keep her from appreciating the workmanship that went into it. The difference was, she supposed, that the Amish made useful things beautiful, while she attempted to make beautiful things that were also, in their own way, useful.

"You were the one who started me on the way to being a crafter," she said, putting in a final stitch and knotting it. "You taught me to crochet before I even started school. Remember?"

Funny how that memory had come back to her—of herself and Rachel sitting at the kitchen table with Emma, the woman's work-worn hands guiding their small ones as they made an endless chain of crochet loops to be formed into pot holders.

"Ach, you remember that." Emma beamed. "You were so tiny, but you caught on fast. Like my own girls."

It went without saying that Amish girls knew such useful things, learning them from their mothers almost before they could talk. Had she and Andrea and Rachel learned anything useful from their mother? Offhand, she couldn't think of anything, unless it was how to evade bill collectors.

"I remember you always welcomed us into the kitchen, no matter how busy you were. You'd find something for us to do." Now, looking back, she knew they'd escaped to the kitchen when her mother was in one of her moods or when their parents were quarreling.

"It made no trouble." Emma had probably known why they were there, but she'd never said. "I liked having you with me for company."

Probably Emma had been lonely, working by herself in the kitchen at the mansion instead of in her own kitchen, surrounded by children, visiting with her mother-in-law while they did the routine chores of taking care of a large family.

"You told us Bible stories." Caro smiled. "Sometimes they came out half in German, I think."

"My English was not so *gut* as the children's. But the stories were the same, whatever the tongue."

"Yes." She supposed they were. "I have a feeling I was a pest, always asking questions. I wanted to know why you wore a cap, I remember."

The prayer cap now covered gray hair, instead of blond, but it was identical to the one Emma had worn then.

"The Bible says that a woman should pray with her head covered, and also that we should pray at all times."

"Do you pray at all times?" The words were out before she could think that Emma might not want to answer so private a question.

But Emma just smiled. "Often enough that I would not want to be taking a cap on and off, for sure. I know the English don't hold with that rule. The praying is the important part, ja. And I pray for you, little Caro."

Her throat tightened. "Thank you. I haven't…haven't prayed so much. Not in a long time. God always seems pretty far away to me."

Emma took a final stitch and bit off the thread. "If God seems far off, it is because we have moved. Not God." She stood, apparently feeling that was all she needed to say about it. "Come. We will have coffee with Nancy."

Heart still struggling with the concept, Caro followed her to the farmhouse kitchen. Nancy sat at the long wooden table, her workbasket in front of her, but she greeted them with a smile and set it aside to get the coffeepot from the stove. The room was filled with afternoon sunlight and the mouthwatering aroma of the sticky buns that sat cooling on top of the gas range.

A faceless rag doll lay atop the basket, hair in braids, awaiting its replica of Amish children's clothing. She picked it up, wanting to think about anything but her relationship with God. "This is lovely, Nancy. Is it for one of your daughters?"

"Ja." Nancy's smile was the thank-you she wouldn't say in response to a compliment. "I had a bit of time after finishing the baking to work on it."

She made sewing the doll sound as relaxing as if she'd taken a nap.

"Do you ever sell them at the local craft shows? I'd think they'd be very popular." They were unique in their lack of features, reflecting the Amish adherence to not making any images.

Nancy shook her head. "We put some out when we have our produce stand in the summer, that's all."

"Would you like to have me take some to the shows on consignment?" She had second thoughts almost immediately. Was she breaking any Amish taboos with the suggestion?

Nancy glanced at her mother-in-law, and Emma nodded. "That would be a fine thing, I think. We would like that, Caroline."

Actually, once they committed to it, both Emma and Nancy showed a lot of enthusiasm for the idea. By the time Caroline was ready to go home, she carried not only her quilt and several Amish cloth dolls but also some carved wooden toys created by the Zook men. And the promise of the loan of a quilt frame so that she could finish her work on the quilt more easily.

She pulled the car into her parking space behind the barn and began unloading. Something else was sticking with her from that visit. Emma had played a huge role in her young life, and she hadn't even realized it until this afternoon.

The memories of that time, which came back more strongly with each day she spent here, proved that. Emma, in her quiet way, had made her feel safe. Secure. Loved. Loved by the Heavenly Father who was such a strong presence in Emma's life.

Emma's words came back to her. If she no longer felt God's presence, was it God's fault? Or hers?

Arms filled with a box containing the dolls and toys, the quilt folded on top, she followed the walk that led around the corner of the barn. It was too much. She wasn't ready to face any tough spiritual questions right now. All she could do was try to get through things as best she could. She—

She rounded the corner and nearly walked into the man who stood at her door.

The bag Caroline was clutching slipped from her grasp, but he caught it before it could hit the ground.

"I'm so sorry. I didn't mean to startle you."

Easy smile; open, boyish face; a disarming twinkle in his eyes. Churchville's mayor—she'd met him at the last craft fair. For an instant she couldn't think of his name, and then it came to her. Keith Morris.

"No problem. I just didn't expect anyone to be here. I don't get many visitors, but that doesn't mean I should overreact when someone comes to my door." She fished her key from her bag, hoping she didn't look as embarrassed as she felt.

"I'm sure it's only natural for you to be edgy under the circumstances." Keith's mobile face expressed concern.

Circumstances? For a moment she imagined he knew about Tony, but that was impossible.

"What circumstances?" She pushed the key in the lock, juggling the packages in her arms.

"Here, let me help you with those." He relieved her of her load so quickly she didn't have time to refuse. "I heard about the vandalism. That's a terrible thing. That's really why I'm here."

"You know something about it?" She could hardly object when he followed her inside since he was carrying her things. She nodded toward the dining room table, and he set everything down.

"No." He looked startled at the suggestion. "No, I don't. I just wanted to apologize on behalf of the town. As mayor, I'm afraid I feel responsible when a newcomer to our little community gets such an unpleasant welcome."

"I could hardly blame the town, could I? But thank you for your concern. I'm sure you have plenty of more important things to do in your position."

"Important?" His right eyebrow quirked. "You do realize that the most significant part of the mayor's role in Churchville is to sign proclamations, declaring that it's Pennsylvania Apple Week, or American History Month. And did you know that this coming week is Community Festival Week?"

She had to smile at the self-deprecation in his voice when he talked about his job. "I'm sure it's more complicated than that."

"A little. I oversee town departments, of course, such as the police department. So I feel a little responsible when our police chief lets vandals run around loose."

"I hardly think it's fair to blame Chief Burkhalter for that." She snapped the words before she could think that it was odd for her to be defending Zach.

"I'm sure you're right." He backed down without, it seemed, a parting glance at what he'd just said. Was telling people what they wanted to hear part of a politician's job?

"Yes, well—" She turned away, appalled at herself for springing to Zach's defense. She didn't owe him that. "I was lucky I didn't have anything very significant in the barn. And believe me, it has a nice, sturdy lock on the doors now."

"Good, good." He rested his hand on the back of a chair. "I have to confess that wasn't the only reason I came to see you."

"No?" She raised an eyebrow, wondering if this was the prelude to a pass.

"I'm interested in the quilt you talked about with my mother. The 1850s one."

She blinked. Did he realize it was one of the things he'd carried in? "I'm pretty fond of it myself."

"I collect quilts—in a minor way, that is. I wondered if you were interested in selling it."

She could only stare at him for a moment. Was this some sort of game he and his mother played to get the price down?

"According to your mother, my quilt doesn't have much historical value." The woman's quick dismissal of her quilt was still annoying.

"I'm sorry about that." Again that boyish smile disarmed. "Mother can be a bit difficult at times. So many people see her as an expert and ask for advice that she just doesn't want to be bothered with it."

"Odd." In her experience, crafters were the nicest people on earth, always willing to help each other. She must be the exception.

"In any event, I think that quilt would be a great addition to my collection. What are you asking for it?"

The usual rule at shows was that everything was for sale if the price was right, but she didn't feel that way about the quilt. "I'm afraid it's not for sale."

"Oh, come on," he said. "Name a price."

She shook her head. "It's a piece of family history."

"One thousand dollars?"

She had to keep herself from gaping. "I'm afraid it's not for sale," she said again, infusing her words with a note of command.

He glanced toward the quilt, lying folded on the table. "Is that it?"

She nodded. Since he'd shown so much interest, she could hardly refuse to show it to him. "Would you like to see?"

"Of course."

He helped her unfold the quilt onto the table. She had to force herself not to say irritably that she'd do it herself. Really, she didn't understand why she was so possessive about the thing.

"There you are."

He took a step back to survey the quilt. "Very interesting. It's an unusual combination of patterns for that time period, from what I know."

"That's what I understand, too." She touched the edging. "Maybe that's why it interests me. I'm trying to research its history, and my grandmother has begun finding some letters and papers that relate to the time period. Hopefully I'll find some mention of the quilt."

He nodded toward one of the torn triangles. "You know, there are people who specialize in repairing and restoring old quilts. If you'd like, I could give you some names."

"No, thanks. I'd prefer to do it myself." She was sure of that, even if she didn't quite understand why.

"But it's a big job—"

"I can manage." Really, what business of his was it if she wanted to do it herself? She'd already told him it wasn't for sale.

"Now I've annoyed you." He gave her a rueful smile. "I'm sorry. I was just trying to be helpful."

"Well, thank you." She hoped she didn't sound too ungracious. "Everyone has been very helpful—I guess

I'm not used to that after living in the city for so long. The Zooks are even bringing over a quilting frame to replace the one destroyed by the vandals."

"That's good. And you said you'd put a new lock on the barn door?"

"My brother-in-law took care of that, but I doubt the vandals would strike twice in the same place."

"Still, better safe than sorry." Keith's smile was a little warmer than friendly. "I'm glad the incident hasn't given you a distaste for our little town."

"Not at all. I'm happy to be here." To her surprise, she realized that was true. In spite of the problems that seemed to have followed her, she felt more at home than she had in years.

"That's good." His smile broadened. "I'm glad."

She couldn't help smiling back. Some simple, un-complicated flirting was a welcome change from dealing with the betrayal hidden behind Tony's smooth facade.

Or with Zach's intensity. A pair of frowning gray eyes appeared in her mind, and she tried, without success, to dismiss them.

"That is such a clever idea." Karen Burkhalter leaned across from her booth at the Spring Festival to take a closer look at the children's activity Caro had set up.

"Since it's a community event, I thought it'd be good. I've done it at this kind of show before, and most kids like to string beads." She'd made a trip to the nearest craft store for supplies for the simple craft, and it had been a pleasant distraction from everything else that was going on in her life.

"You're really getting into the swing of things here."

Karen's pert, freckled face lit with a smile. "I'm glad. That means you want to stay."

Karen's insight startled her. Was her attitude that obvious? "I guess I am enjoying it here." But for how long?

"They're opening the doors," Karen said. "Get ready to be swamped."

She didn't really expect that, but over the next hour it looked as if Karen's prediction would come true. People flooded through the aisles between the booths, locals and visitors alike. She should have realized that it would be difficult to supervise the children's activity and deal with adult customers at the same time.

She was trying to untangle the mess one overeager ten-year-old had made of her necklace when someone slid around the table and into the booth with her. She looked up to see Andrea.

"You can use an extra pair of hands." Andrea shoved a strand of blond hair behind her ear and took the string of beads from her. "I'll do this. You take care of the customers."

"I…thank you. I didn't expect this."

Andrea, who managed to look crisp and businesslike even in jeans and a button-down shirt, deftly untangled the beads. "Rachel would have come, but she was too busy at the inn. Hey, it'll be fun."

It would? She enjoyed it, but it hadn't occurred to her that Andrea might. There was a lot she didn't know about her sisters, it seemed. She turned to a woman who wanted to argue her down on the price of the Amish dolls.

"Well, I don't know if my grandkids would like them. Don't you have any with faces?" She picked at the fine hand stitching on the doll's dress, and Caro had to restrain herself from snatching it away from her.

"It's handmade by an Amish woman," she said firmly. "Amish dolls don't have faces because the Amish don't believe in making images of people. If you want a cheap machine-made doll with features, I'm sure you can find that somewhere else."

She held her breath. She didn't usually turn away customers, but she wouldn't insult Nancy by selling her handmade dolls for less than they were worth.

"I guess you have a point at that." The woman looked over the display. "I'll take four of them."

She managed to keep a straight face until the woman had paid and walked away, and then she turned to Andrea, a laugh escaping. "I can't believe I just did that."

"You sounded like my husband. Cal feels the same about his handmade furniture. If you want cheap machine-made, go elsewhere." Andrea, having a moment's respite from the demands of the children, leaned against the table. "You know, you really have a feeling for Pennsylvania folk art. Maybe that's what you're meant to be doing."

The idea startled her. First Karen, now Andrea pointing out something she hadn't seen in herself.

Andrea glanced over her shoulder. "Looks as if you have another customer."

Caro turned, and her breath caught. The woman who stood on the other side of the table wasn't a customer. She was Tony's wife.

"Mrs. Gibson." Caro said the words with a sense of fatality. Of course the woman would seek her out. What else could she do? She should have seen this coming.

"I thought you were claiming that name." The woman's tone was combative, but Caroline saw past that to what lay beneath. Grief. Despite what he'd done to her, Mary Alice had loved Tony.

"What do you want?"

"To talk, that's all. You can spare me a few minutes, can't you?"

Caro glanced around. They couldn't talk here, not in the midst of the crowd. "Andrea, can you take over for a few minutes?"

Andrea nodded, controlling the questions that no doubt seethed in her mind.

Caro slid out of the booth, struggling to find composure. She had to do this. She didn't want to.

Please. She wasn't sure whether it was a prayer or not, it had been so long. *Please show me what to say to her.*

"Let's go out back. Maybe we can find someplace quiet to talk." She touched the woman's arm. Mary Alice winced away from her, but she followed when Caro started down the aisle toward the rear of the fire hall.

They got there too fast. She hadn't come up with anything to say by the time she pushed through the metal door and went out to the gravel lot.

The area around the door was piled with boxes left there by the exhibitors, and a couple of pickups were parked nearby, but there was no one around. It was as private a place as they were likely to find in the midst of the festival.

She turned to the woman. "I guess this will have to do. I'm sure you don't want to come back later."

"No. Let's get this over with." Mary Alice's thin face tightened. She'd probably been a beauty once, with those soft curls and huge brown eyes, but years of tending a child and an ailing father-in-law had taken their toll.

For an instant Caro felt an irrational fury at Tony. What right had he to betray this woman—to betray both of them? Hadn't he had any sense of morality at all?

"How did you find me?"

The woman shrugged. "Your friend told Tony he was police chief here. I stopped at the station, asked for you. The guy on duty said you'd probably be here."

Simple, wasn't it? "All right, what can I tell you?"

"You told my father-in-law that you were Tony's wife." Mary Alice folded her arms across her chest, as if holding back pain. "What did you mean by that?"

"I wasn't trying to hurt you or him. I wanted to find out—"

"Are you after what Tony left?" Mary Alice blurted out the question. "Because if you are, you're going to be disappointed. He didn't leave a thing, and if he had, it would belong to me and his child."

The thought of that child was a fresh source of the pain she'd thought she was finished with. "No. I don't want anything. Just the truth."

"The truth is that Tony was my husband. Maybe not a very good one, but mine." Her thin cheeks flushed. "You have no right to say anything else."

"I'm sorry. I thought I was married to Tony." She tried to harden her heart. She had her own pain to deal with. "We got married in Las Vegas. But if you two were never divorced, then it was all a sham."

"I don't believe you." The woman's face was taut with pain. "Tony wouldn't do that. We were married in the church. He might do a lot of things, but not that."

Caro fumbled in her shoulder bag and pulled out the photo she still carried around. She should have gotten rid of it. Having it was like biting down on a sore lip, but she hadn't been able to bring herself to throw it away.

"Here." She held the image out to the woman. "Is that your Tony?"

Mary Alice took the photo, hand trembling. Looked at it. Shoved it back toward Caro, turning away. Her shoulders shook with sobs.

"I'm sorry." Her voice was thick, too. She grabbed the picture, taking a brief glance at the smiling bride and groom, and shoved it back in her bag. "I didn't want to hurt you. But I was victimized by Tony, too."

Mary Alice took a deep, rasping breath. She turned back to face her, clearly still fighting for control. "Sorry. I thought—"

"I'd have thought that, too, in your place. But honestly, I don't want anything that was Tony's."

Mary Alice wiped tears away with her fingers, managing a weak smile. "Good thing. As far as I know, he didn't even leave enough to bury him. I guess you did that."

"Yes." A fresh twinge of pain hit at the thought of the tears she'd shed at the graveside. Not only wasn't she Tony's widow, but she couldn't even be sure Tony was dead.

She pushed that thought away. Someone had sent that safe-deposit key, but that didn't mean it was Tony. A thought hit her. If that money had been come by honestly, it would belong to Mary Alice and her child.

"I'm not sure if this is going to help you, but when I came to Philadelphia, it was to check out a safe-deposit box that Tony had rented. It was filled with money."

Something that might have been hope dawned in the woman's eyes. She hated to squelch that, but she couldn't let her believe that her money troubles were over.

"The police out in Santa Fe think Tony might have been involved in something illegal, so don't get your hopes up."

"Hope?" Anger flared in Mary Alice's voice. "What do you know about it? Hope doesn't feed a kid or put shoes on her feet."

"I know how you must feel, but—"

"You don't know anything about what I feel. Don't you dare feel sorry for me. At least Tony actually married me. What does that make you?"

Before Caro could say a word, she'd whirled and raced away.

Caro stood there for a few minutes, dealing with the emotions that boiled up and threatened to explode. She didn't have the luxury of collapsing in tears or even kicking a few of the stacked boxes. She had to pin a smile on her face, go back inside and take over her stand. So that's what she'd do.

The crowds seemed to have thinned out as she moved through them to the stand. Maybe most people had gone outside to the food stands and the rides. Andrea sent her a questioning look.

"Everything okay?"

She summoned a smile. "Fine. Do you want to take a break? I can manage."

"Maybe a little later." Andrea gestured toward the children's table. "I still have a few customers."

Caro glanced at the four children grouped around the table. Three flaxen heads—common in this area with its

German heritage. And one little girl with curly dark hair and an engaging smile. Ruthie, Zach's daughter.

He wouldn't like the fact that Caro was anywhere near his little girl. He'd made that clear at the last show. But what could she do about it? She could hardly chase the child away.

Even as she had the thought, the little girl lifted the necklace she was working on. "It's pretty, isn't it?"

Since Ruthie was looking right at her, she could hardly avoid answering. "It sure is. Are pink and purple your favorite colors?"

She nodded gravely. "My daddy says they're princess colors. My princess doll has a dress that color."

"Your daddy will really like your necklace, I'm sure."

"Someday I want to make pretty necklaces like yours." Ruthie leaned across the table and reached up to touch the aqua and silver cross Caro wore. "It's be-yoo-tiful."

Karen, overhearing, grinned at her niece. "I'll bet you could ask Daddy to get one just like that for your birthday. Maybe Ms. Caro would even make it, wouldn't you?"

"Well, yes, of course, if he wanted me to." It wasn't Karen's fault that she was in such a sticky situation. Karen didn't know that her brother's only interest in Caroline was that of a police officer.

She turned away, relieved, at the sight of a potential customer, and went to the other end of the booth, switching places with Andrea, determined to stay as far away from Zach's daughter as possible.

Once she'd persuaded the woman that she shouldn't pass up the earrings that went with the necklace she wanted, the other three children had wandered off to look at something else. To her surprise, Ruthie still bent over her necklace, totally absorbed in stringing beads on the cord.

Her sketching pad, never far away, lay on the corner of the table. A pencil in her hand was usually a sure remedy for thinking about things she'd prefer to ignore.

Her gaze was drawn back to the little girl, and the pencil started to move. She didn't have quite the angle she wanted, so she edged closer quietly, not wanting to distract the child. She didn't want to talk to Ruthie— she just wanted to capture the intent look an artist, no matter how young, had when absorbed by the work.

She didn't know how much time passed before she realized someone was watching her—had probably been watching her for some time. She looked up to find Zach leaning against his sister's booth, his gaze fixed relentlessly on her face.

Her heart seemed to skip a beat and then proceed to thud too loudly. Foolish, but she couldn't seem to ignore the effect the man had on her.

"Your daughter decided to make a necklace." He could hardly blame her. The activity was open to any child who wanted to do it.

Ruthie looked up at her words. "Daddy, Daddy!" She launched herself into his arms.

"Hi, sweetheart." He caught her, his face lighting with a love that made Caro's breath hitch. "What are you doing?"

"Making a necklace, see?" She scurried to hold it up for his inspection. "It's all finished. Isn't it pretty?"

"It's beautiful." The pink-and-purple creation dangled from his strong hand. "I'm proud of you."

"Ms. Caro showed me how." Ruthie turned to her,

and her gaze touched the sketch pad. Her eyes widened. "Is that me?"

Caro nodded. And what exactly would Zach think of that?

He took the pad, his fingers brushing hers, and turned it so that he could see. It seemed to Caro that his face gentled. "Look, Ruthie. It is you."

While Ruthie exclaimed over the image and called her aunt Karen over to see, Zach's gaze met hers. For once there was nothing guarded in it.

"You've really captured her. That expression of total concentration—I've seen that so often, always when she's making something."

"You have an artist on your hands," she said lightly. She tore the sketch carefully from the pad and handed it to him. "For you."

"Thank you." His voice was low, and she couldn't seem to look away from his gaze.

After a long moment, Zach turned away. He took Ruthie's hand. "Say thank you to Ms. Caro, honey. We'll find Grammy and show her what you made."

"Thank you, Ms. Caro." Velvet brown eyes sparkled, and a pair of dimples flashed in her cheeks. "I love your necklaces."

"You're welcome, Ruthie. I'm glad you came." She would not let her confused feelings for Zach affect the way she treated the child. "I hope I'll see you again."

Zach wouldn't like that, she supposed. Well, too bad.

He gave her a slight smile, raised one hand in a sketchy salute and walked off with his daughter.

TWELVE

All Ruthie could talk about for the next several hours was her new friend, Ms. Caro. Zach eventually turned her over to his mother at home, still chattering, and headed back to the festival.

They'd be closing down now, and he'd take a quick look around the grounds to be sure everything was all right. And if he saw Caroline, well, that was inevitable, wasn't it?

The bond that had started to form between his daughter and her Ms. Caro would be a nice thing to see, if only Caro were not involved in who-knew-what.

She could be perfectly innocent of any wrongdoing. But even so, he didn't want his daughter around someone who seemed such a magnet for trouble.

Caroline knew that. He'd seen it in her eyes when she looked at him.

He didn't like the thought that his attitude hurt her. She'd been hurt and betrayed enough. But that was all the more reason to be cautious of any relationship with her. Duty came first for him, and that duty could very well cause him to do something that would hurt her still more.

All very good reasons for staying away from her. So

why was he headed straight for the spot where her booth had been?

His sister was already gone. One of his brothers must have stopped by to help her pack up.

Caroline seemed to be down to several boxes that looked ready to take out. He stopped behind her as she picked up one.

"Can I give you a hand with those?"

The box she balanced wobbled in her arms at the sound of his voice, and he grabbed it. "Sorry. I didn't mean to startle you."

"That's fine." She tightened her grip on the box. "I didn't hear you coming. Thanks, but I can manage these."

"No point in making two trips when one will do," he said. He picked up the rest of the boxes. "Lead the way."

Her brow furrowed, as if she were about to argue, but then she shrugged. "My car's out back."

They made their way to the back door, sidestepping folks tearing down their booths. "The festival had a good turnout." He addressed her straight back, since that was all that was visible to him. "The craft shows have become quite a draw for tourists. How did you make out with the things you brought on consignment for the Zooks?"

She looked at him over her shoulder. "How did you know about that?"

He shoved the door open, holding it with his shoulder until she maneuvered her box through. "I hear just about everything, it seems."

"I guess that's a valuable trait for a police officer. Everything sold pretty well—the dolls in particular. I think Emma and Nancy will be pleased." She crossed the gravel lot to her car and opened the hatchback. "Everything should fit in here. If I keep on with the craft shows, at some point I'll need to borrow a bigger vehicle."

He wedged the last box in on top of the things she'd already loaded and closed the hatchback. "There you go. What happened to your sister? She didn't hang around to help you tear down."

"She had a Saturday-night date with her husband, so I chased her off home. I can manage the unloading myself."

"No need. I'll follow you home and help you unload."

Her mouth tightened infinitesimally. "You don't have to do that."

"I want to." He turned toward the side lot where he'd left his car. "I'll be right along." He walked off before she could launch into an argument.

The few minutes it took to drive from the fire hall to Caro's barn were enough time to wonder what he was doing. Not, unfortunately, enough to come up with an answer.

Caroline was already unloading by the time he pulled in behind her car. He thought she was going to reiterate her insistence that she could handle this herself, but instead she gave him a thoughtful look.

"Maybe it's just as well I have a chance to talk to you. I had a visitor today. Tony's wife."

Her expression didn't tell him how she'd taken that. "I suppose that was inevitable. How did it go?"

She shrugged as she headed for the door. He picked up a stack of boxes and followed her.

"Not very happily, as you might imagine. She…well, I guess she needed to vent her anger at somebody."

"What happened wasn't your fault." He held the door while she carried her load inside and then followed her. "If she's going to be angry, Tony ought to be her target."

"Unfortunately, he's not around to hear what we think of him." She crossed to the worktable and set her stack of boxes down, so he did the same.

"What did you tell her?"

"She didn't really want to hear anything from me. I did tell her about the money, though." She swiveled to face him. "Of course, I don't know if it's still there. Did the police take it?"

"Not that I know of." At her skeptical look, he held out his hands. "I'm not in the confidence of the Santa Fe police. I told them about it, as you asked me to. They haven't kept me posted on their plans."

He could guess, but they hadn't told him. If it were his case, he'd probably leave the money where it was to see if anyone showed an interest in it.

"And if they did tell you, you couldn't pass anything along to me in any event."

"No, I guess I couldn't. So where does that leave us?"

"Destined to talk about something else, I suppose. Your daughter is adorable."

As a change of subject, it was a good one. "I think so, but I might be prejudiced."

"The proud father." Her smile seemed to relax. "I can understand that."

"You had a nice activity for the kids today. Not many of the vendors bothered to do that."

She moved into the kitchen and began putting coffee on, seeming to assume he'd stay. "Maybe they didn't think of it. I've been at other shows where vendors have had kids' activities. Or had displays of work in progress. That always seems to draw an audience."

"You enjoyed participating in the show." He didn't really need to ask. She'd been completely wrapped up in what she was doing.

"I did, yes." She leaned against the counter, waiting for the coffee to brew. "I'd gotten away from the craft-show circuit when I was working at the gallery. Francine always seemed to have so much going on that there wasn't time for anything else."

"What kind of things?" He put his elbows on the breakfast bar countertop, curious about what her life had been like in Santa Fe.

"Charity events, for the most part. Francine's late husband, Garner, was very active in the social scene in Santa Fe, and running charity auctions was something he'd started. She got involved and then carried it on after his death." The coffeepot clicked, and she lifted a couple of mugs from the shelf. "I was busy so many Saturdays that I got out of the craft-show circuit. Besides—"

"What?" He liked that she was talking to him so easily, as if they were friends.

She shrugged. "Much as I love the Southwestern art, there's just something about Pennsylvania folk art that speaks to me. It feels so familiar."

"It's part of your childhood, even if you got away from it for a while." He wrapped his hand around the mug she shoved toward him. "Sometimes I think I should be trying harder to keep Ruthie's Afghan culture alive for her, but I'm not sure how to do it. And her parents were Christian, so they were already isolated from their culture to some extent."

"I didn't realize." She leaned on the counter opposite him, so that they were close but with a barrier between them. "How old was she when you brought her back here?"

"Four. She still has some memories, mostly of her parents. I hope she doesn't remember the fighting."

"Were her parents killed?" Her voice was very gentle.

He nodded. It wasn't easy, even after all this time, to think about that. "They were both doctors, doing good work in an isolated area of Afghanistan, but there was a lot of prejudice against them because of their faith. When our team was sent there, we got to know them pretty well."

"How did they—" She stopped. "I'm sorry. I shouldn't bring up something so painful."

His fingers tightened on the mug. "It's okay. The good Lord knows my memory of that is never very far away. What happened to them was my fault."

"Zach—" Her voice was troubled.

He shook his head. "Sorry. I didn't mean to sound melodramatic, but that's how I see it. I left my post because a car overturned in front of me and I ran to help. The terrorists were waiting for that—they got into the village and attacked the clinic. David and Miriam were both killed. Thank goodness Ruthie survived."

Her hand closed over his. "I'm so sorry you lost your friends. But anyone would have done the same."

"Maybe. But if I'd stayed at my post, they'd be alive today."

"You don't know that."

He shook his head.

"Zach—" Her fingers moved comfortingly on his hand. "If something I did made you think about it, I'm sorry."

"Not your fault." He turned his hand, so that he clasped hers. "I guess it was seeing her so absorbed in making that necklace. Her mother loved to make things, too. She'd do these little crafts with Ruthie whenever she had the time. Seeing her like that reminded me of Miriam."

"They'd be proud of the way you're raising their daughter."

"I hope so."

"I know so." Her mouth curved in a smile. "Anyone can see how she adores you."

"The feeling is mutual." He smiled back at her, and somehow those smiles seemed to touch a deep well of understanding. Her green eyes darkened with aware-ness. But she didn't look away.

The moment drew into an eternity. And then he leaned across the counter and kissed her.

Her lips were soft under his, and she made a small sound that might have expressed surprise. Then she leaned into the kiss, reaching up to touch his cheek with her fingers.

The counter was a barrier between them. Maybe that was just as well. It forced him, eventually, to pull back.

Caro's eyes were soft, almost dazed. He touched her hair, and one of those wild curls tangled around his fingers, seeming to cling with a mind of its own.

He couldn't do this. He drew back, shocked at himself. "I'm sorry. I shouldn't have."

She turned away. "No. I mean…we shouldn't. It's not a good idea."

It wasn't. But that didn't keep him from wanting to kiss her again.

So probably he'd better go before he got himself into any more trouble.

* * *

Caroline folded the quilt carefully, wrapping a sheet around it. She'd come to the house for a family dinner and couldn't resist showing off the repair work she was doing on the antique quilt. "I've actually found references to a quilt Elizabeth was making. I'd like to believe it was this one, although there's no proof, of course."

"It's like a treasure hunt," Andrea said. She folded napkins, setting the table with the same efficiency she used to prepare a spreadsheet. Rachel's Tyler had come up from Baltimore for the weekend, and she was busy in the kitchen, having chased the others out to the breakfast room to set the table. "I wonder if there are any other primary sources. Journals, other letters, family histories—that sort of thing."

"I hadn't thought of that." Caro carried a stack of Grams's favorite Lenox plates to the table. It was far better to keep herself occupied with the mystery of the quilt rather than let her mind stray to Zach and that kiss.

He'd known immediately that it was a mistake. They both had. Why did she find it upsetting that he'd been so quick to admit that? She knew as well as he did that there couldn't be anything between them.

"Caro?"

She blinked, jerking her mind back to the present to find Andrea looking at her questioningly.

"Sorry. My mind was wandering. What did you say?"

"I asked if you wanted me to do an Internet search to see if I could locate any other information."

"That would be great. As it is, it's like listening to only one side of the conversation. If only I had Elizabeth's letters to her sister, instead of just her sister's to her."

"That would be pure gold if I could find that," Andrea said. "And about as rare. But let me take a look and see what I find."

"Are you talking about the quilt?" Grams carried a pitcher of daffodils to the table.

"If it is the same quilt, and that's a big *if,* Elizabeth's sister mentions getting the pattern for her from a Reverend Albright. You wouldn't expect a minister to be passing on quilt patterns."

"Maybe it was from his wife." Grams tweaked the blossoms. "I think everything is ready in here. Do we dare interrupt Rachel to see if she's ready?"

"Not I," Caro said quickly. Rachel was the mildest of creatures, but she could turn violent if interrupted in the midst of culinary creation.

"Nor I," Andrea said quickly.

Caro grinned. "Up to you, Grams."

Grams gave a ladylike snort. "I'll get her."

But the kitchen door popped open, and Rachel burst through carrying a laden tray. "Where are the men? The food is ready now."

"We're here." Cal's voice sounded from the hallway. He never strayed far away from Andrea, she noticed. Tyler loomed behind him, and Rachel's gaze caught his.

Something clutched Caro's heart. Surely she wasn't jealous, was she? Her sisters deserved to find happiness with good men who loved them.

It was just that she felt…bereft, she supposed. Not at the loss of Tony, but at the realization that what she'd imagined they'd meant to each other was an illusion.

There was no one for her, and she was left standing on the outside, watching her sisters' happiness but unable to share it.

Rachel carried platters to the table, and for a few moments all was confusion as she and Andrea brought the rest of the food, filled water glasses and finally took their places around the long table.

Grams reached out, and they all linked hands around the table. She'd forgotten, in all those years away, that family custom. Rachel held her hand on one side and Andrea on the other. She could almost imagine she felt love flowing through the link as Grams asked the blessing on the meal and on the family.

They loosed hands at the Amen, and platters began to fly around the table—fried chicken, baked corn, fluffy mashed potatoes, the relishes that were characteristic of a Pennsylvania Dutch dinner.

"Rachel, you've outdone yourself." Cal took a biscuit and passed the basket to Grams. "This is wonderful."

"Well, she had an incentive," Andrea teased, with a sidelong glance at Tyler. "Tyler was coming."

Tyler grinned. "Then you should thank me, right?"

"I guess so." Andrea took a forkful of mashed potatoes and looked at Grams. "Can we tell Caro yet?"

"Tell me what?" She couldn't help a spasm of apprehension. Most of the surprises in her life had not been happy ones.

"I suppose we'd better, since you've given it away," Grams said.

"What?" Surely they wouldn't all be smiling at her if it were bad news.

"We've seen how much you love dealing with the local arts and crafts," Grams said. "So we thought a good addition to the bed-and-breakfast would be a crafts shop in the barn. Which you would run, of course."

She could only stare. "But…that would be very expensive, renovating the barn, getting the stock. I don't have any cash to put into a project like that."

Thanks to Tony. If he hadn't wiped her out, this might be a possibility. But if he hadn't, she might never have come home and realized that what she wanted was right here.

"Your contribution would be your expertise," Andrea said. "Grams will front the start-up costs with the settlement she received from the embezzlement of Grandfather's business. And I'm sure I can get you a small-business loan for whatever else we need."

Her mind whirled with possibilities, and for a moment she let herself hope. "But the renovations—"

"You have a carpenter and an architect right in the family," Tyler said. "I've already drawn up some preliminary plans, but Cal and I need your input. We thought you might want some space for craft classes and groups to meet."

She tried to combat the tears that welled in her eyes. "I can't let you do all this for me. It's too risky. There are other craft and gift shops…."

"You have access to Amish-made crafts that many others don't." Grams smiled, her eyes soft with tears. "Emma loves you as if you were one of her own children."

"She mentioned the idea to begin with," Andrea said. "Rachel and I just took it and ran with it."

"So, Caroline." Grams smiled through her tears. "What do you say? Will you do it?"

She couldn't speak. Couldn't say anything in the face of this overwhelming love. She could only nod and put up her hands to try and stem the tears that over-flowed, washing away the barriers that remained between them.

Zach had stayed away from Caro for several days, trying to forget that kiss. It hadn't worked. Still, he'd managed to rationalize it to a certain extent.

They were attracted to each other, and they'd had a moment of closeness that took them both a little too far. More serious for him than for her. There was no actual investigation going on, so he hadn't violated any regulations, but he knew in his heart that was a cop-out.

Attraction or not, he had a responsibility to check on her. Santa Fe PD might not want to involve him in their investigation of Tony Gibson, but he wouldn't ignore the odd things that kept happening in Caroline's vicinity.

At least, that was what he told himself when he pulled up to the side door of the inn. He wanted to touch base with Rachel. If she could talk her stubborn sister into moving into the house, he'd feel a lot better about Caroline's safety.

But when he tapped at the door nearest the kitchen, it was Emma who answered. "Morning, Emma. Is Rachel around?"

"She has gone to New Holland for groceries. Is there some way I can help you, Zachary?"

Emma had moved to a first-name basis with him when her son had been injured last year.

"It's nothing important. I'll catch her later. What about Caroline?"

"Ach, she is not here, either. She has gone to the airport to pick up her friend who comes for a visit."

That was the first he'd heard of a friend coming. Someone from her life in New Mexico? Maybe someone who knew Tony? "Was that her friend from Santa Fe?"

"Ja, the lady she worked for out there. I have the blue bedroom all ready for her."

"Guess it wasn't my day to find anyone home. Stay well, Emma."

She nodded, shutting the door.

That was a pointless trip. Still, it was interesting to learn that her employer was coming. Francine Carrington—the woman who'd reported her missing.

He went down the steps, glancing toward Caroline's apartment, and came to a stop. Caroline might not be there, but someone was. He caught sight of a flicker of blue, maybe a shirt, disappearing around the corner of the barn.

Could be nothing. Could be the person who'd been in the apartment a couple of times, back for another try.

He glanced toward the patrol car, but it would be faster on foot. He jumped lightly off the patio and ran across the grass.

Better this way, in any event. The prowler, if that's what he was, would hear a car coming. This way, he'd catch him unawares.

It worked out just about that way. He rounded the end of the barn, moving quietly on the grass instead of the path, and there the man was, looking in the window.

"Police. Stop right there and turn around."

Somehow he wasn't entirely surprised when the man turned around. Jason Tenley, supposed photojournalist. He hadn't bought that from the moment he'd met the man.

"Just looking for Ms. Hampton, Chief. That's all."

Tenley held his hands up, palms toward him, as if to show he wasn't holding a weapon.

Not that he expected a weapon. If the prowler had intended harm to Caro, he wouldn't do it by making coffee.

"Looking in her window?" He shook his head. "You'll have to do better than that, Mr. Tenley. Suppose we go back to my office and talk about it."

Tenley looked chagrined. "You're not really going to arrest me, are you? I suppose technically I'm trespassing, but…"

"*Prowling* was the word I had in mind," Zach said. Something was off-key here. The man wasn't reacting the way he should be, having been caught by the police.

"Guess maybe it's time to come clean." Tenley tried a disarming smile.

"It wouldn't hurt." He wasn't disarmed.

"I'm not a peeping Tom. I'm an insurance investigator. Let me reach into my pocket, and I'll show you my ID."

Zach gave a curt nod. Insurance investigator. The words sounded more reasonable than the photojournalist bit.

Tenley handed over an ID folder. Zach studied it and then slid it into his pocket.

"You won't mind my hanging on to this until I check it out."

"Wouldn't do any good arguing, would it? Especially since I'd like your cooperation."

"It's a bit late for that."

"I guess it looks that way from your viewpoint."

"From any cop's viewpoint." The guy might be legit, but that didn't mean he was letting him off easily. "If you come into my jurisdiction on an investigation, you ought to know enough to check in with me. Now, why are you here?"

And what did it have to do with Caroline?

"You're right. I shouldn't have tried to take a short cut. The truth is, my company is on the hook for a substantial sum over a charity auction in Santa Fe, and they're not eager to advertise the fact that they've been had. A very expensive piece of Native American jewelry that was donated for the auction has turned out to be a skillful fake."

He didn't need the man to connect the dots for him. "Caroline Hampton was, I assume, the jewelry expert on the gallery's staff."

Tenley nodded. "She's the only one, so far as we've been able to determine, who had the skill to make such a convincing switch."

"I take it you don't have any actual evidence, or this would be coming from the police."

"That's about the size of it." Tenley ran a hand over his graying hair, then massaged the back of his neck. "It's been a real headache. Both the owner and the insurance company want to keep this a private matter as long as there's a chance of regaining the object."

"And what progress have you made?" He wouldn't let himself focus on the Caroline he'd grown to know. He couldn't.

"Precious little." Tenley spread his hands. "Ms. Hampton hasn't made a suspicious move since she's been here. Only thing that might have caught my attention was that trip to Philadelphia, but since she went with you, I assume she wasn't contacting any fences."

"No." He was tempted to hold the man until he'd

checked out his story, but that would be more a product of his own irritation than good police work. "Where are you staying, Mr. Tenley?"

"White Rose Inn, out on the highway."

"All right." He gave a curt nod. "Stop by my office tomorrow afternoon. I'll have checked this out by then. In the meantime, stay off this property. We clear?"

"Right." If Tenley was relieved, he didn't show it. "I'll be on my way."

He went quickly, rounding the end of the barn at a lope. A moment later his car bounced out the lane toward the road. Zach watched, automatically noting make and model, license number.

Now what? Go back to the office, check out the story Tenley told.

It would check out. Tenley wouldn't make up something so easy to disprove. And then—well, then he was going to have to tread very carefully.

He'd begun to have feelings for Caro. But those feelings could explode and hurt both of them if she wasn't the woman he thought her to be.

On the other hand, if she was innocent in all this, she'd feel betrayed when she learned he'd been investigating her. And she'd been betrayed too many times in her life to forgive that again. There was no possible happy ending in all of this that he could see.

THIRTEEN

"Now we're getting into typical Pennsylvania Dutch country." Caroline nodded toward the dairy farms spread across the rolling landscape. Once she'd picked up Francine at the airport in Philadelphia, she'd been eager to get off the interstate and out into the country again.

"Very pretty." Francine barely turned her expensively coiffed ash-blond head to glance out the window.

"You didn't look," Caro accused, half laughing.

It was good to see Francine again, but rather odd, too. They'd had a good relationship, a friendship even, but she'd always been aware of their employer/employee relationship.

Francine gave an elaborate sigh. "Really, Caroline. You should be aware that I'm not a scenery person."

"True. I've never known anyone who was more urban than you." Even in Santa Fe, where most people gloried in the magnificent outdoors, Francine had looked slightly too sophisticated to fit in.

She'd been surprised that Francine hadn't gone back to her native San Francisco after her husband's death, but she'd been devoted to running the gallery and continuing Garner's charities. There had been rumors of a suit launched by Garner's children from his first marriage, contesting his will, but Francine had never mentioned it.

Francine touched her hand. "Now you know how much I care about you, to be willing to spend time in this rural wilderness. I suppose there's not even a decent coffee bar in this small town of yours."

"Well, no." She tried to imagine one of the stolid Pennsylvania Dutch farmers picking up the latest mocha cappuccino before heading out to do the milking. "But my sister makes a fine cup of coffee."

How long would Francine last here? Probably not for more than a few days, but she was touched that Francine would make the effort at all.

"I'll defer judgment on your sister's coffee until I've tasted it, if you don't mind. Now tell me. Has anything more happened with regard to Tony?"

She'd been keeping Francine up to date at her insistence, so there wasn't much new to tell. "Not since I talked with you after we found out about that safe-deposit box and Tony's wife. Believe me, that was enough of a shock to last quite a while."

Francine frowned for an instant and then smoothed the frown away, always careful to preserve her flawless complexion. "I'm not sure it was a good idea to take the local cop along on that expedition. Why tell the police something they don't already know?"

"He's all right." She pushed the memory of that kiss away. "Anyway, I could hardly hide the existence of all that money. If Tony was involved in something illegal, I don't want it in my possession."

"I suppose not. But as for that first wife—well, darling, he should have told you about her, but I refuse to believe there wasn't a divorce. Tony was hardly the type of man to commit bigamy."

She had to smile, even though the situation wasn't humorous. "Is there a type of man likely to do that?"

"You know what I mean." Francine dismissed that with a wave of her hand. "I'm relieved nothing else has happened. Perhaps whoever was playing games has tired of it."

"Maybe." She wasn't convinced she was at the end of this trouble, but maybe she was just being pessimistic.

"So, are you about ready to give up your rural solitude and come back to Santa Fe where you belong?"

"I don't think so." She couldn't imagine how Francine was going to take her news. "As a matter of fact, my family wants me to create and run a crafts center and shop in conjunction with the inn."

Francine's head swiveled to give Caro the full effect of a disbelieving stare. "You're not going to tell me you're settling in here for good."

"Well, maybe not forever. But for the foreseeable future, anyway."

To her surprise, Francine didn't jump into telling her what she should do, as was her usual practice. Instead she turned back, to stare absently at the winding road ahead for a long moment.

"Much as I hate to say this, maybe that's the best thing for now."

An odd note in her voice set Caro's nerves on alert. "What do you mean?"

"That's really the reason I came." Francine didn't

seem to want to look at her. "I hate to be the bearer of bad tidings, but I feel as if I have to warn you."

"Warn me about what?" Her hands tightened on the steering wheel.

"Something happened at that last charity auction we ran." Francine's voice was slow. Reluctant. "There was an elaborate turquoise and silver pin—an original design by a noted Zuni artist. Do you remember it?"

"Yes, of course I remember it. I set up the display and did the photographs." She'd held the beautiful thing in her hands, marveling at the artistry and craftsmanship, knowing that however good she was, she'd never make anything that perfect.

"The new owner had it valued. It's a fake."

Her head spun. "How could that be? I worked on it. I know it was genuine. It was checked out by the insurance expert before it went on display. Surely they don't think that the gallery had anything to do with the fraud."

"Not the gallery," Francine said. "You."

Caroline narrowed her eyes, trying to make out the sign that was nearly hidden by a rampant growth of wild roses. It would be hard enough to see in the daylight; in the dusk it was nearly impossible. She had to come to a stop to read the sign, and even then it wasn't reassuring. She wasn't supposed to be on Twin Forks Road, was she?

She'd followed Emma's directions to reach the Stoltzfus farm and arrived there without incident. Even now, several carefully wrapped quilts rested on the backseat, ready to be shown in the craft center once it opened. Now getting back home was the problem.

Maybe she was jumping the gun, collecting materials for the shop while it was still in the planning stages, but she wanted to be sure she had enough inventory to give her new project a chance of success.

Besides, it had been a distraction from the bad news Francine had brought with her when she arrived three days earlier. Since then they'd gone over the counterfeit backward and forward, exploring every possibility, without coming to any conclusion.

Francine had reiterated her support a number of times, but Francine was also concerned for her gallery's good name. She wouldn't sacrifice that for the sake of friendship, and Caro didn't want her to. But where did that leave her?

She hadn't been able to bring herself to tell her grandmother and sisters about this new complication. How long could she expect even their support to last?

Grams would say that there was Someone who was always there to support her. Emma had said that if God seemed distant, it was because she had moved away, not God. Maybe that was true, but if it was, how did she bridge that gap?

Lights flashed in her rearview mirror and she looked up, startled. Apparently she wasn't the only one on this lonely road. Good. It felt a little less isolated. It must lead somewhere, hopefully to a road whose name she'd recognize before it was completely dark.

The driver behind her came up fast—too fast on this narrow road. His lights reflected in her eyes, and she flipped the rearview mirror to diminish the glare. Irritation edged her nerves. If he was in that much of a hurry, why didn't he just pass her?

She eased ever so carefully closer to the side. There could be a ditch or a drop-off, hidden by the lush undergrowth. She raised her hand to motion him around—

The car rammed her, snapping her neck back and taking her breath away. Shock ricocheted through her, and she stepped on the gas in an automatic reflex.

The car surged forward, but he was right on her tail, bumping her again and sending the car fishtailing before she regained control. Crazy—he had to be crazy.

She clutched the wheel, hunched forward as if to ward off a blow, pressing down on the gas. *Please, please. Help me.*

No hills to deal with, thank goodness, but she went shrieking around the bends blindly, terrified that she'd meet someone coming, but at least then she wouldn't be alone out here with a maniac on her tail—

He came up fast, lights glaring, and rammed her again. She fought the wheel, but it did no good, she couldn't regain control, she was losing it—

The car spun dizzyingly and plunged off the road. Her body was thrown backward, then forward as the car lurched to a stop in a mass of rhododendron bushes. The airbag deployed, muffling her. For a moment she couldn't move, couldn't even assess whether she was hurt.

But she had to move. She could hear the other car, coming back toward her, engine roaring. She had to get out, now, before he reached her.

She fumbled with the seat belt, freeing herself, shoving at the folds of the airbag, and slid across to the passenger door, shoving it open, clambering out.

Taking a quick glance toward the road, she saw the

car stop, a dark figure get out. No time to see more; she just ran. Into the dark, anywhere away from him.

She stumbled through the undergrowth, brambles tearing at her clothes, and then burst into the woods where dry leaves rustled with every step.

She couldn't worry about being quiet—he was too close behind her. She rushed through the woods blindly, panic harsh in her throat, breath dragging painfully.

She'd gained a little on him, hadn't she? She could hear him crashing through the underbrush. Stop. Think. Once he got in the clear he'd overtake her easily.

She looked around, eyes adjusting to the dimness. There—that clump of trees surrounded by bushes. If she could get in there before he came any closer, she could hide.

Please, please. She ran to the bushes, threw herself on her stomach and squirmed her way beneath, reaching back to ruffle the dry leaves so that she'd leave no telltale traces.

Just in time. She could hear him now, closer, so close she could hear the ragged gasps of his breath.

She curled into a ball, hiding her face against her knees. *Please, Lord. Please. If You're there. If You hear me, protect me.*

The footsteps came closer, crunching the leaves. A low chuckle chilled her bones. Did he see her?

A whisper, so soft it might have been a flutter of birds' wings. It came again, a little louder.

"Caro." A whisper, just on the edge of hearing. "Caro, come out. Come out."

She pressed her face tight against her knees, clenching her teeth. He knew where she was, she would feel a hand grabbing her, dragging her out—

He turned. His feet rustled through the leaves, going back toward the road.

She let out the breath she'd been holding. *Wait, wait, don't move yet, not until he's farther away.*

Finally she couldn't hear him any longer. She crawled out. Don't go toward the road, he could be waiting. The other way—that was the only safe thing. She moved slowly, cautiously, one step at a time.

Nothing. If he heard her, if he was coming, she'd know it. She hurried blindly through the woods, away from the road, falling, getting up, running, falling again, until finally she was in a field, the stubble of grass under her feet, and ahead of her the lights of a farmhouse.

The brightness of electric light, not Amish, then. They'd have a phone. She started toward the house at a staggering run. She was safe.

Thank You. Thank You.

Zach sent a cautious glance toward Caroline as he drove down the lane from the Miller farm to the main road. "Are you sure you don't want to stop by the E.R., just to be on the safe side?"

Caro shook her head, reaching up to lift a strand of hair away from the bandage that adorned her forehead. "You heard Mrs. Miller. Nothing but bumps, bruises and abrasions."

"Margo Miller is used to patching up three accident-prone sons, but that doesn't make her a doctor."

She turned her head slightly to smile at him. "I'm all right, really. I just want to go home."

"If you're sure." His stomach had been tied up in knots since he got the call from John Miller that Caro had turned up at his door. It began to ease, just a little, at the smile. "Have you thought of anything else about the car?"

She moved restlessly. "We've already gone over all that."

They had, but he suspected she needed to talk it out before she reached the inn. "Sometimes something else comes back once the initial shock has passed."

"I didn't really get a good look—just lights in my rearview mirror." Her voice tightened on the words, as if she didn't want to relive those moments.

"What about when you got out of your car? Did you try to see where the other vehicle was?"

She glanced toward him, her breath catching. "You're right. I did. It was just a dark shape, but I'm sure it was a sedan. I guess that doesn't help much."

"It eliminates all the pickups in the county," he said lightly. "We might find something when we go over your car. When he rammed you, he might have left a paint chip that would tell us the color."

"I didn't think of that." She shook her head. "I haven't been thinking of much of anything, to tell the truth. Just…scared."

"That's not surprising." It took an effort to keep his voice level when he thought of her in danger out on that lonely road. "You're entitled after what you went through. Any chance you got a look at the driver?"

"It was dark. I couldn't see anything about him." Her voice tightened, alerting him. There was more, he was sure of it.

"Notice how he walked? Did he give the impression of a young man?"

"I didn't see him, I told you."

"Hear him, then. Did he speak?"

Her hands twisted together in her lap. This was it. She'd heard him.

"Not to say 'speak.' He…whispered."

He wanted to reach out, to cover those agitated fingers with his, but he couldn't. "What did he whisper?"

"My name." Her voice was the whisper now.

"You're sure?"

At her nod, his jaw clenched. It wasn't a random thing, then. He hadn't really thought it was, but there was always a chance. He glanced at her.

"There's something else, isn't there?"

She held out against the question for a moment, and then she nodded. "He didn't say Caroline. He said Caro." Her fingers twisted again. "Tony called me that. He… I didn't believe he could be alive. But who else would know?"

She sounded at the end of her rope, and for a moment he couldn't think of her as a suspect, only as someone he cared about, someone who was hurting.

"I don't think you can assume that." He tried to keep his feelings from sounding in his voice. It wouldn't do either of them any good to let her know he cared. "Your sisters call you Caro. I've heard them. Probably a lot of people around here have."

"I suppose." She didn't sound convinced.

He could hardly blame her. The bottom line was that the attack on her wasn't a random thing, so whether the attacker was Tony or someone else, this situation had taken a turn to the dangerous.

They were almost at the inn, and once her grandmother and sisters saw her, to say nothing of her friend, he wouldn't have a chance to say anything in private.

"Look, I want you to promise me something."

She looked at him. "What?"

"Promise me that you'll stay at the inn tonight, okay?"

She nodded. Her eyes were wide and frightened in the intermittent illumination of the streetlamps. "That's not a permanent solution. Why is this happening, Zach?" Her voice choked on a sob. "I have to know."

He did reach out then, clasping her hand briefly in his. "I wish I could answer that. But I won't stop looking until we know the truth. I promise."

FOURTEEN

Caroline turned away from the stove and nearly tripped over Barney. When she'd made it clear she was returning to the apartment the next night, Grams had insisted that if she wouldn't listen to reason, she'd at least take the dog along for protection.

"You'll take care of me, won't you, sweetie?" She ruffled Barney's silky fur, and he gave her a foolish grin and a soft woof.

She was afraid Grams didn't understand her insistence on coming back to her own place. It wasn't about asserting her independence, not anymore. She loved and trusted them.

Just as important, she'd taken her first step toward trusting God again last night. Funny. She'd wrestled with how that would happen, and then when it came, it had been as natural as breathing.

She walked into the living room, carrying her mug of coffee, and Barney padded at her heels. Much as she'd learned to love this place, it did seem lonely with darkness pressing against the windows. But she hadn't really had a choice. Danger was coming closer, and she wasn't going to let it get anywhere near her family. She'd face it here.

Barney put his head on her knee, as if he sensed that her thoughts were getting too grim. She petted his head. "Sorry. I guess I'm not very good company, am I? Maybe if I talk to you, I can keep from thinking about what happened last night."

But she couldn't. She kept hearing that voice whispering her name. She'd heard it last night, too, but at least she'd had the comfort of Rachel's soft breathing in the other twin bed to help block it out.

Caro. No one in Santa Fe had called her that but Tony. Still, Zach was right. Plenty of people here had heard the nickname. Even Zach had used it once or twice. Wasn't it more rational to assume that the dark figure was someone, anyone, other than Tony?

She was thinking too much again. She took a sip of the coffee and made a face. Why on earth had she made coffee? It would keep her up all night. Not that she expected to do much sleeping, in any event.

Barney's ears pricked, and he raised his head, giving a soft woof. A knock at the door followed a moment later.

The dog didn't act as if it were a stranger. She went to the window nearest the door and drew the curtain back. Her sisters stood on the doorstep.

She'd thought this was settled. She opened the door, trying to look perfectly calm and confident.

Before she could say a word, Andrea had elbowed her way in, arms laden, with Rachel right behind her.

"Since you won't come to us, we've come to you," Andrea announced. She tossed a couple of sleeping bags on the rug in front of the fireplace. "We're going to have a pajama party."

"Andrea, Rachel—" She choked up before she could say anything else.

"Don't argue." Rachel carried her bundles to the kitchen. "We have the makings of a first-class pajama party—brie, crackers, fruit, my special panini sandwiches, hot chocolate and marshmallows, the works."

Andrea grinned. "Doesn't sound remotely like any pajama party food I can remember."

"Well, I trust our palates are a little more sophisticated now." Rachel moved from stove to countertop to refrigerator as if she were perfectly at home. Maybe, for Rachel, any kitchen was home.

"I hope Tyler knows what a treasure he's getting." She crossed to the breakfast bar.

Andrea followed her. "She reminds him with every meal. I'm sure when Cal faces one of my meals, fresh from the deli, he thinks he's married the wrong sister."

"I had first shot at Cal, you'll remember, and he never got past looking at me as a little sister." Rachel turned the heat on under the hot chocolate pot and slapped a fry pan onto the front burner. "He took one look at Andrea and he was a goner."

Andrea's smile was tender and reminiscent. "He didn't act that way. Spent most of his time yelling at me for one thing or another, as I recall."

"He adores you, and you know it." Caro looked from Andrea to Rachel. "You're lucky, you know. Both of you, to find such good men."

Andrea gave her a quick hug. "Baby, it's going to happen for you, too. Just because Tony turned out to be a jerk—"

Rachel made a soft murmur of dissent, but Andrea shrugged that off.

"Don't give me that look, Rach. We all know the man was a con artist if not something worse, and Caroline deserves way better than that." She glanced at Caro's face. "Okay? Or would you like to slug me?"

That surprised a laugh out of her. "Tact isn't your strong suit, is it? But you're right. It's just taken me a while to accept."

Rachel turned a sandwich. "I can understand that. It's one thing to accept something intellectually, but another to really get it in the heart."

Caro could almost feel the tension drain out of her. "How did I get two such wise older sisters?"

"It took us a while." Andrea's expression grew serious. "We let you down. We know that now. We were both so eager to get away from Mom that we didn't think about what it was going to be like for you, left alone with her."

Tears welled in Caro's eyes. It was far more than she'd ever expected to hear from Andrea, who was always so sure of herself. "It's okay." She forced the words past the lump in her throat. "Really."

"Okay, enough serious stuff." Rachel slid plates in front of them, then turned back to get the platter of brie, grapes and crackers. "Wrap yourself around that, and I guarantee you'll feel better. Prosciutto, goat cheese, roasted red peppers, sautéed mushrooms—"

"And your secret sauce?" Andrea teased.

Caro took a bite, the flavors exploding in her mouth. "Wow, Rachel. This is prize-winning food. You're right. This would bring a dying man back from the brink for one more bite."

"Oops, almost forgot." Andrea turned to scrabble through her bag. "I brought something that's going to cheer you up almost as much as Rachel's food." She put a sheaf of fax papers onto the countertop. "My Internet research paid off faster than even I expected. I found a family historian in Boston who is writing a history of Elizabeth's family. And—wait for it—he actually had some of Elizabeth's letters written to her sister from Pennsylvania."

Caro put down her sandwich. "You're kidding! How on earth did you find him that fast?"

"Genealogy sites." Andrea smiled, a little smugly. "You'd be amazed at what's out there, and most of the serious researchers are eager to share. He faxed these when I promised to send him photos of the quilt and any additional information we find."

"Hurry, look at them," Rachel urged. "Andrea wouldn't let me get even a peek. She said you had to be first."

Caro bent over the faxed sheets, deciphering the faint, faded script. It had become easier since she'd been reading the letters from Elizabeth's sister, and she was able to go through them fairly quickly, reading out pertinent bits to her sisters.

"Listen to this." She frowned at the page. "She says, 'I have completed the quilt according to the pastor's instructions, and I eagerly await the first opportunity to put it out.' That's a little odd, isn't it?"

"Maybe she just means to use it," Rachel said, scooping up melted brie with a cracker.

"Could be." But something was niggling at the back of Caro's mind—something she'd read or heard, that had to do with quilts.

"Listen to this one." Andrea had picked up another of the sheets. "This really is odd. She says, 'Thank you, my dear sister, for your concern. I am upheld by your prayers. As you say, this venture can be dangerous, but when I think of the perils of those we help, our dangers are nothing. If only I could be sure who to trust. A Friend was taken into custody two nights ago, and all are praying for him and questioning who could have betrayed him.'"

"Wow," Rachel said again. "I always pictured women of those days living a pretty quiet life. Sounds like Elizabeth had something more serious on her plate. I wonder what it was."

"Well, my new genealogy friend promised me more letters in a few days, so maybe the answer will be there." Andrea looked toward the stove. "Are you going to give us some of that hot chocolate, or just let it steam away over there?"

"Goodness, I forgot." Rachel scrambled to get the hot chocolate served up, along with a shoofly pie that she said was Emma's contribution to the party.

Between the food and the lively chatter her sisters put up, Caroline realized to her surprise that she actually wasn't worrying any longer. She had a new life, and plenty of new things to occupy her mind. With so much support, she'd get through this dark time.

They cleaned up together, chattering in a way she couldn't remember since they'd been children. Her sisters had grown into women to be proud of. Andrea, so smart and efficient, but with a new softness about her since she'd come back home and met Cal. And gentle Rachel—there was strength behind that gentleness that surprised her.

What did they think of how she'd turned out? She wasn't sure she wanted to know. She'd certainly made more than her share of mistakes.

They finally settled in front of the fireplace with refills of hot chocolate. "I guess we should have asked your friend to join us," Rachel said. "But she went out to dinner, and I didn't like to interfere with her plans."

"You mean you thought she'd put a damper on the party," Andrea said, smiling.

"It's just as well," Caro interceded. "I don't think Francine is the pajama-party type." And Francine certainly didn't have to tell Caroline where she was going for the evening, although she was a little surprised that she hadn't.

"It was nice of her to come here to support you," Rachel said.

"It was. She's bravely doing without her gourmet coffee for the sake of being here for me."

"I did manage to fix some hazelnut this morning that she said wasn't half-bad." Rachel's grin said that she wasn't offended.

Andrea stretched. "Look at the time. I'd better get some sleep. I'm supposed to meet with a new client in the morning."

Caro was about to say that they could go and sleep in their own beds when the noise came. Rachel froze, half into her sleeping bag, and stared at the back wall—the one the connected to the barn. "Did you hear that?"

"How could you help but hear it?" Andrea demanded. "Somebody knocked something over. Sounds like your vandals are back, Caro." She was already dialing her cell phone. "Cal, there's someone in the barn. Yes, all right. We will, just hurry."

She snapped the phone shut. "Cal says to stay inside and keep the door locked. He's on his way, and he's calling Zach."

When Caro would have moved, Rachel grabbed her. "It's all right. They'll be right here. Cal was staying in the house tonight. It'll only take a couple of minutes."

"I don't have a couple of minutes." Caroline pulled free and headed for the door, seized by a compulsion she didn't really understand. "I can't wait. Don't you see? The quilt is in there. Vandals—" Words failed her, but the pictures filled her mind—some ignorant kids slashing at the quilt, stretched on its frame, throwing paint at it—

She reached the door and grabbed the flashlight that hung next to it. Barney, excited, jumped at her heels, barking. "I'll be all right. I'll take Barney—"

"We'll all go." Andrea coolly pulled a poker from the fireplace rack. "It's our history, too."

"Right." Rachel rushed to the kitchen and returned brandishing the fry pan. "Let me at them."

Caro's fear was swept away by the desire to laugh. "All right. Let's go."

She opened the door. Barney ran ahead of them, barking wildly. How they must look, running after the dog in the dark. The fear she'd felt the night before in the woods was a distant memory. She could take on anything with her sisters behind her.

They rounded the corner of the barn. Barney gave a fierce bark, followed by snarling and snapping, and a man's frightened cry. She swung the torch's beam wildly, trying to focus on the melee.

The dark figure—was it the man from last night?— tore free of the dog and started to run.

But there was no place to run. The police car surged down the lane, siren wailing, just as Cal, breathing hard, burst out of the path from the house.

The man froze, caught in the converging beams of the headlights and the torch. Zach got out of the police car and came toward him.

"Out kind of late, aren't you, Mayor?"

The man turned, full into Caro's light. Keith Morris stood there, and in his arms was the antique quilt.

Zach led Keith to a straight-backed chair in the barn apartment and planted him in it, none too gently. In his opinion, Keith should be sitting in the police station right now, but he'd given in, partly because of Keith's frantic appeals to be allowed to explain, but mostly because Caroline said she wanted to hear him. After what she'd been through, she deserved to hear.

At the moment Caroline and Rachel had spread the quilt on the table and were going over it, stitch by stitch, to be sure it hadn't come to any harm. Andrea had given up her poker, a little reluctantly, and now sat in the corner on the sofa, her husband's arm around her.

"Okay, Keith." He frowned down at Churchville's mayor. "Let's have an explanation. Breaking and entering, theft—those are plenty serious charges."

"No, no, you can't arrest me." Sweat broke out on Keith's forehead, and his gaze swiveled from side to side and settled on Caroline. "You have to believe me.

I just wanted a look at the quilt, that's all. I wanted to know what you had before I made an offer. But then I heard the dog barking, and I ran without thinking."

"You expect us to buy that? You could have come to Caroline anytime and asked to see the quilt if you were interested in buying."

"He already saw it," Caroline said. "He offered to buy it."

"I…I hardly got more than a glimpse then." Keith looked at him and quickly away. "I mean, I thought the price would go up if I showed too much interest—she'd already turned me down once."

"If all you wanted was to look at it, why did you take it out of the frame?" Andrea leaned forward; apparently unable to stay out of it any longer. "You were trying to steal it."

Keith shied away from the words. "I couldn't help it. I mean, it was my mother." He looked up at Zach again. "You know what she's like. She's so proud of being the final authority on things historical in the area, proud of her ancestors being First Proprietors, going back to William Penn and all that. She couldn't take the idea that someone might have something of more historical significance than she does." He sat up straighter, apparently gaining confidence from this line of argument, which just might be closer to the truth.

"So you decided to steal the quilt for her?" He let skepticism weigh his voice.

"Not steal, no. I thought if I showed it to her, maybe she'd decide it wasn't that great and lose interest. Or if not, I'd return it, come to Caroline, make her a fair offer. I thought I'd have it back before anyone even knew it was missing. You don't want to arrest me for that. Think of the ugly publicity."

That was the wrong argument to use on him. In his book, no one was above the law. Maybe it would be tough to go up against the Morris family, but—

"That's not why your mother wants the quilt." Caroline walked toward Keith, her gaze fixed on him.

Zach took a sidestep that put his body between them, shocked by the wave of protectiveness that surged through him. "What do you mean?"

She didn't veer from her focus on Keith, and she spoke to him as if there were no one else there. "You don't know what we found out. We already had Elizabeth's letter from her sister. Now we have copies of the ones she wrote."

Zach shot a glance toward Andrea, who seemed like the one most likely to give him a sensible explanation.

"The Elizabeth Unger who made the quilt," she said. She turned her attention back on her sister. "Go on, Caro. What did you figure out?"

"Elizabeth talked about making the quilt according to the directions she'd been sent. About putting it out for its first use. About a Friend being betrayed and arrested, and how their courage was nothing to that of the people they were trying to help." She turned toward the others then, her eyes alight with excitement. "Don't you see? I remember reading about it—some scholars believe that quilts were used as signals on the Underground Railroad, guiding escaping slaves to safe houses."

"This area was one of the major routes." Everyone knew that. There was even a historical tour of Underground Railroad sites.

"Elizabeth was a perfect person to get involved—

deeply religious, coming from Boston, which was a center for the abolitionist movement." Caroline went on as if he hadn't spoken. "The Friend she talked about…the word was capitalized because she literally meant Friend, one of the local Quakers who were part of the network. She said someone in the area betrayed him to the slavecatchers." She swung back on Keith. "That's what your mother didn't want me to find out."

He'd become so involved in her story that he'd almost forgotten about Keith. Now he saw that the man's face had blanched.

"What about it, Keith? Time to stop dancing around the truth."

"One of your mother's prized ancestors was the traitor. That's it, isn't it?" Andrea was on her feet now, shaking off her husband's restraining arm. "You're trying to save your family reputation."

Keith shook his head helplessly, sagging in the chair. "Mother knew the family stories about it. When she heard about the quilt, heard that Caroline was going to display it, was looking into the history—she thought it was all going to come out. She wouldn't let me alone about it. She said I had to destroy the quilt, make it look like vandals had broken in, anything. I didn't want to, but I couldn't help it."

Zach planted his hands on his hips. "And what about the rest of it? Breaking into this apartment, forcing Caroline's car off the road last night."

Cal cleared his throat, the sound breaking through Zach's fury. "Much as I hate to sound like the attorney I used to be, Chief, don't you think you ought to caution him before he answers that question?"

The words restored his common sense. He was appalled at himself. He was letting his feelings for Caro get in the way of his duty.

He reached for Keith's arm. "Come on. Let's continue this down at headquarters."

"No, no, don't." Keith shrank away from him. "I don't need an attorney. I didn't do anything else, I swear it. I heard about her troubles, but it wasn't me. And I couldn't have done anything last night—you should know that. I was at the town council meeting. It went on until nearly eleven. The council members will tell you. I was there the whole time."

"I won't press charges."

The quiet statement had him swiveling toward Caro. "What are you talking about? He's admitted it."

"But he didn't do the other things. I never thought he did."

No, she wouldn't have believed it could be that easy. Besides, she believed Tony was still alive. "We caught him red-handed running away with that quilt in his arms."

"We got it back. There's no harm done." For a moment she looked ready to burst into tears. "I don't want the trouble it would cause."

"That's not an excuse for not doing your duty." Now it was as if they were the only two people in the room. She knew how he felt about duty. And why.

"Your duty. Not mine." She looked immeasurably tired. "If I don't press charges, you can't arrest him, can you?"

"No. He can't." Keith straightened. "I'm very grateful, Caroline. I hope you won't—"

"That's not all." Now it was Rachel. He'd always thought her the gentle one of the sisters, but at the moment she had fire in her eyes. "There's a condition to not pressing charges."

Zach's gaze crossed with Cal's. Cal gave a rueful shrug. "I suggest both of us contract temporary deafness. Whatever she's going to propose, we shouldn't hear."

That was probably good advice, but he couldn't pretend none of this ever happened.

"You resign." Rachel said, the tone of her voice allowing no wiggle room. "It's in the paper tomorrow, or we press charges. And you and your mother walk on eggshells around us from now on. No more tricks, no gossip, nothing."

"I agree. Anything. Everything." Keith was practically babbling in his efforts to get this over with. "I'll do it."

Rachel glanced at her sisters. She must have seen agreement in their faces. "That's it, then."

He watched, fuming, as Keith gave them all a vague, meaningless smile and bolted from the apartment. He couldn't arrest him if they wouldn't press charges. He resented having the decision taken out of his control. His duty—

"Relax, Chief." Cal nudged him. The sisters were hugging, half laughing, half crying. "It wasn't done according to the book, but at least my wife isn't going to jail for braining the mayor with a poker, Caroline knows the story of her quilt, Rachel got her licks in and Keith is losing the thing that's most important to him. Besides, you're getting rid of the worst thorn under your skin who ever took office in the township. It might not be according to Hoyle, but seems to me it worked out pretty well."

"Not according to the law."

Cal shrugged. "The law has its limitations. I'd rather see justice."

It wasn't his interpretation of doing his duty, but clearly he could do nothing about it. He went to Caro. "I'll be leaving, then."

This wasn't over, not by a long shot. Keith might be removed from the running, but Caro was still in trouble, whether she knew it or not.

"Thank you." Her green eyes glistened with tears when she looked at him.

"You're welcome. I hope the three of you know what you're doing."

He thought about the possible charges hanging over her in regard to the museum theft. She'd been generous to Keith. He suspected the insurance investigator wouldn't be generous toward her.

Zach sat in his office the next afternoon, scowling at the day's issue of the *Churchville Gazette*. True to his word, the announcement of Keith's resignation appeared prominently on the front page. Keith must have run straight home and called the paper to make the deadline.

He tossed the paper aside. Maybe Cal had a point, but he still wasn't satisfied. He had a duty that Cal didn't, and he didn't like being finagled out of doing it for the sake of convenience.

He ignored the phone ringing in the outer office, shoving his chair back. He knew what was really sticking in his craw. He'd let himself start to care about Caro Hampton against his common sense, against his professional duty, against everything he knew was right and sensible. He'd told her more about himself than he'd told anyone other than family, and look where it had gotten him—compromising his duty for a woman who obviously didn't return his feelings.

Eric Snyder opened the door without knocking and poked his head in. "You'd better take this call, Chief. It's the Santa Fe police."

Zach glared at him. "I've got it. Shut the door. And hang up."

He picked up the phone, waiting until he heard the click that told him the line was private. "Chief Burkhalter here."

"Chief. This is Charles Rojas. We spoke a while back about Tony Gibson and his widow."

"I remember, Detective." The neutral tone of his voice must have alerted the man that he wasn't feeling particularly cooperative. They'd pretty much told him to buzz off, hadn't they?

"Yes, right," Rojas said quickly. "And you were real helpful, sending along that sketch of Leonard Decker the way you did."

He grunted. That hadn't seemed to lead anywhere, as far as he could see.

"Ms. Hampton still there, is she?"

"Yes." He sat up straight. Something was going on. Santa Fe PD hadn't called him just to chat. "What about it?"

"We just found his body."

He clutched the receiver, mind working feverishly. If Leonard Decker was dead in Santa Fe, it was highly unlikely he'd been running around this part of Pennsylvania trying to make Caro believe her husband was still alive. "When?"

"That's the thing." The tone of the detective's voice

told him there was bad news coming. "He's been in the river, but the ME pegs the time of death as somewhere around the same time Ms. Hampton left Santa Fe. We consider that an interesting coincidence."

"If you're suggesting that Ms. Hampton killed him—" He stopped. He wouldn't do Caroline any favors by alienating the investigator. Not that he could do her favors in any event. His duty was all he could do. "Do you know anything about the forgery of some jewelry at the gallery where she worked?"

He could almost sense the interest on the other end. "How do you know about that, I wonder? Have you been holding out on us, Chief?"

"I might ask you the same thing, Detective." This was his jurisdiction, after all.

Rojas paused. "Okay," he said finally. "We've been hearing rumors, but no one is talking—not the gallery people, not the victim, certainly not the insurance investigators."

"One of the insurance investigators is here. Keeping an eye on Ms. Hampton. He claims she had the expertise to make the switch, but no proof."

Rojas whistled softly. "Told you more than they have us, then."

"He had to. I was about to arrest him for trespassing."

"That'll do it, all right." Rojas chuckled. "Look, Chief, seems to me it's time for us to put our cards on the table. Maybe we can help each other."

And who will help Caroline? The voice at the back of his mind was insistent, but he managed to silence it. If she was innocent, Caroline would only be helped by finding out the truth. And if she was guilty—

If she was guilty, his feelings had nothing to do with it. He'd do his duty.

"I'm listening," he said.

FIFTEEN

Caroline stood by the barn doors, watching as the movers carried the remnants of her life in Santa Fe into the barn. With a new lock once again installed by Cal and with Keith frightened off for good, her things should be safe until she had the heart to go through them.

She fidgeted restlessly as box after box was carried inside. Who would have thought she had so much stuff? If she'd packed it herself, she'd have gotten rid of things, including most of Tony's belongings. As it was, she'd simply taken what would fit in her car and left the rest to the movers. They'd have packed everything down to the Sunday paper and the cans of tuna fish in the cabinet.

Tony's things rightfully belonged to Mary Alice now. Would she want them? That was yet another hurdle, one she didn't want to face.

Speaking of facing things, maybe she ought to admit what was really bothering her. Not the task of sorting through her old life. It was the fact that she hadn't seen Zach since the night before last, when they'd exposed Keith's activities.

She should have realized she was treading on his devotion to duty when she took matters in her own hands and settled with Keith. But didn't he see that she and her sisters had done him a favor? If it had come down to the chief of police arresting the mayor, it would have been a three-ring circus. No one could predict how something like that would turn out. Zach might have been the one to suffer most, not that he'd let that stop him.

She sensed movement behind her and turned to see Francine picking her way along the path gingerly as if it were lined with snakes. She wore capri pants and a snug top with a pair of high-heeled sandals that were inappropriate anywhere outdoors.

She teetered to a stop next to Caro. "I see your belongings have finally arrived. It might have been faster to have sent them by mule train."

Caro shrugged. "I suppose. I wasn't in any hurry to get them. It just means I have to sort everything out."

"No need to rush into doing it." Francine touched her lightly, sympathetically, on the arm, surprising her. Francine wasn't a touching person, generally. Caro had never seen her hug anyone other than her late husband or a potential big donor to one of her charities.

Hearing Francine voice what she'd just been thinking made her reconsider. "Thanks, but I'd better face it. After all, Tony's things don't really belong to me."

"If you believe that hick sheriff knows what he's doing." Francine's tone made it clear that she doubted it.

"Police chief, not sheriff," she corrected, a little pang reminding her that she was unlikely to be talking with Zach on that subject, or any other, anytime soon.

"At least that business with the quilt has been cleared up." Francine seemed to be looking for something to distract her from that rather sad parade of belongings.

"The things these small-town folks don't get up to. Imagine committing robbery to cover up something that happened 150 years ago."

"If someone threatened to expose something harmful about Garner's family, you'd jump into action quickly enough."

Francine stiffened a little at the mention of her late husband, but then she smiled and shrugged. "Believe me, I'd find a better way of dealing with it. A little blackmail goes a long way in some circles."

"Maybe so. Keith isn't as sophisticated as you."

"You're convinced he wasn't the man who forced you off the road? Maybe your police chief was too quick to accept that alibi."

"Not my police chief. And no, it couldn't have been Keith, unless he has an identical twin no one knows about. He was in full view at a town council meeting all evening."

"Well, I suppose it'll sort itself out." Faint lines appeared between Francine's brows. "If there is any chance it was Tony, that's another reason not to do anything about his belongings, you know."

"I suppose so. But I hate having this unfinished business hanging over me. And, frankly, I'm not sure I owe Tony any kind of loyalty at this point."

"But, Caroline—" She stopped, because a familiar police car was pulling up behind the moving van.

Zach got out, very stiff and correct, dark glasses hiding his eyes. Something in her tensed as he approached. If only he'd let her explain why she'd intervened with Keith, maybe she could clear that air between them.

"Zach." She forced a cheerful note into her voice. "You remember my friend Francine Carrington."

He gave Francine a curt nod and turned back to her.

"I'm afraid I'll have to ask you to come down to the police station with me."

She blinked. "Look, if this is about Keith again—"

"It has nothing to with that."

"What, then?" She couldn't keep her voice from rising. "What's going on? You're scaring me."

A tiny muscle twitched at his jaw, the only acknowledgment of her words. "You need to come with me now. Two detectives from Santa Fe will be arriving shortly to question you."

She heard Francine's sharp, indrawn breath. She didn't seem to be breathing at all. "Question me about what? Tony?"

"About Leonard Decker. The man you said threatened and harassed you."

"I've already told you everything about that." Why are you doing this? That was what she wanted to say. Why are you looking at me as if I'm a criminal?

"He's been found. Dead. He was murdered about the time you ran away from Santa Fe."

She was vaguely aware of Francine murmuring that she'd get her sisters and hurrying off toward the house, teetering a little on her heels. Silly, to notice that at a time like this.

And then all she could feel was the iron grip of Zach's hand on her arm as he led her to the police car.

They filled up Zach's tiny office at the police station— she, Zach and the two officers from Santa Fe—one short and burly, the other tall, young, almost elegant in his Western dress. She felt as if they were using up all the air in the room, leaving none for her.

"Now, Mrs. Gibson, you must see that it's in your best interest to be honest with us." The younger one was smooth and persuasive.

"Hampton." That was all she could think of to say. "We—I found out that Tony had a wife in Philadelphia he hadn't bothered to divorce before he married me."

That probably only increased their suspicion of her, but she was too tired to think what was the best thing to say. If Zach, who knew her, could believe her capable of murder, what chance did she have of convincing anyone else?

Zach. The pain cut deeper than any she'd ever known, even deeper than the knowledge of Tony's betrayal. Maybe that was because she'd always suspected, at some level, that Tony wasn't honest. Zach was a man of integrity. If he believed this, maybe she really wasn't worth being loved.

Zach moved slightly in his chair. "Ms. Hampton has not been apprised of her right to have an attorney present."

The detective shot him a look of dislike. "I'm sure Ms. Hampton would rather have a friendly talk with us than a formal interrogation with an attorney present."

What Zach would have said to that she didn't know, because the door opened and Cal burst in. Zach shot to his feet. "Burke, you're not licensed to practice law in Pennsylvania. Get out."

"I'm not, but I've brought someone who is." He ushered in a graying, distinguished-looking man who reminded her in some way of Grandfather. "Caro, this is Robert Hanson. He's an old friend of your grandparents' and he's your attorney. Don't answer any questions unless he tells you to." Cal bent to press his cheek against hers before anyone could object. "It's going to be all right," he whispered. "We're all waiting outside and praying for you."

"Out." The older of the detectives grabbed Cal and shoved him out of the office. He grinned and gave her a thumbs-up as he went.

The ice that encased her began to thaw. They were here. They were taking care of her. Even Zach, in his way, hadn't let them bully her into talking without an attorney. Maybe somehow she was going to get through this.

There were moments when she doubted that, over the next two hours, when the wrangling between Hanson and the detectives turned into a blur of noise that made her dizzy. When that happened, she clung to the thought of them—her family, waiting for her.

Someone else was here with her. *Draw near to God, and He will draw near to you.* She'd looked for a reference to what Emma had said in the Bible she'd found on her bedside table. Those were the words that expressed Emma's thoughts perfectly. *Draw near to God, and He will draw near to you.*

She listened to the attorney and answered only the questions he allowed, convinced that those questions made no sense. She'd never spoken to Decker before that day in the plaza, never heard Tony mention his name. She didn't know what Tony had been involved in. He'd lied to her from the first time she met him.

Maybe her voice had trembled on that, because the

attorney's hand had closed warmly over hers, as if it were Grandfather there next to her.

"I think that'll be all Ms. Hampton will answer today," he said.

The detective lost his urbane charm, leaning toward her with a quick, threatening movement. She didn't think she reacted, but Zach was between them in an instant.

"You heard the attorney. Now either you're going to charge Ms. Hampton or let her go."

"Stay out of this, Burkhalter. This is our case."

"This is my jurisdiction." Zach's voice carried no expression at all, but it was like a door clanging shut. "Charge her or let her go."

"Of course Chief Burkhalter knew perfectly well they didn't have enough evidence to charge her." Robert Hanson leaned back in the leather chair that had once been her grandfather's, accepting a mug of coffee from the tray Emma held. They'd all come back to the library at the inn for a council of war once she'd finally been released. "He's a good man to have on your side, my dear."

She could only stare at the man from her place on the couch between her sisters. "I don't think he is."

"Listen to Mr. Hanson," Cal advised. He took a tray of sandwiches Emma had put on the table and began forcing them on people. "That could have been a lot worse if Zach hadn't been looking out for your rights."

Her rights. Yes, she supposed Zach would do that for anyone. It was part of doing his duty. She suddenly felt an overwhelming urge to cry.

She got to her feet, drawing startled glances. "I…I know we have to talk this over, but I can't seem to think.

I need to take a hot shower, change my clothes, and then maybe I'll be able to eat something."

Cal glanced toward the attorney. "Maybe we'd better get this over now, Caro. Mr. Hanson has a busy schedule."

But Hanson waved with a thickly piled ham sandwich. "Not at all. I'll just sit here and catch up with Katherine. Take your time, my dear. I know the atmosphere of suspicion can seem to contaminate you when you're not used to it."

Andrea and Rachel stood up, one on either side of her. "We'll go with you," Andrea said firmly, and took her arm.

All she wanted was to be left alone to let the tears out, but she knew she'd never get rid of them that easily. She let them walk with her back to the apartment, trying to nod and smile at their attempts to distract her.

Once Rachel had run a hot tub, more relaxing than a shower, she insisted, and Andrea had laid out a change of clothes, she shooed them toward the door.

"I can handle the rest of it," she said firmly. "I know how to take a bath by myself. I'll come back as soon as I feel a little more together. You go now and keep those two lawyers from scaring Grams with their stories, all right?"

Her sisters exchanged glances. "She has a point," Andrea admitted.

"Maybe we are hovering a little," Rachel said. "All right. But if you're not back in an hour, we're coming for you."

"I will be. Go." She shoved them out the door and locked it behind them.

The confident manner only lasted until the door closed. She had to drag herself back up to the loft. She peeled off her clothes, tossing them to the back of the closet. Maybe she'd throw them away.

Only when she lay back in the tub did the tears come. Whatever they might say about Zach defending her, she knew things were over between them. She'd known all along it couldn't possibly work, but she hadn't been able to quash that tiny flicker of hope. Well, now it was gone for good.

She sat up, sloshing water over the tub. How ridiculous was this, hiding away to cry while people who loved her made plans for her defense. She wasn't a child who needed protection, much as she appreciated what they were trying to do.

The familiar urge to run had disappeared completely, she realized with surprise. She'd grieve, and go on grieving for the loss of whatever she might have had with Zach, but she wouldn't run. She'd stay and face this.

She got out, dried herself, made up her face and brushed her hair free of tangles. Then she put on the clothes her sister had laid out and went down the stairs.

They'd be surprised to see her back so soon. Well, she was surprised, too. But it was time she started acting like one of the grown-ups.

She opened the door, stepped outside and turned to shut it. She sensed movement behind her, felt a fierce pain in her head and then slid into blackness.

SIXTEEN

Zach leaned back in his chair, leveling a gaze at Rojas, the senior of the detectives. The past hour had been an exercise in futility since Caroline left, surrounded and supported by friends and family.

Not by him. He'd done what he could for her, but it hadn't been enough.

Doubt had been growing in him throughout the endless afternoon. If you followed the rules, you got the right result. That was what he'd always believed, but it didn't seem to be working out that way this time.

Where is the truth in this, Lord? Help me to find it, whatever the cost.

"Let's stop the posturing, Rojas. It's pretty obvious you don't have anywhere near enough evidence to charge Ms. Hampton in Decker's death. What's this really about?"

Williams, the younger man, opened his mouth for what would probably be another jab at hick cops, but Rojas waved him to silence.

"Go out there and get the dispatcher to give you a cup of coffee."

Williams gave him a mutinous look, but he went.

When the office door closed behind him, Rojas spread his hands wide.

"Okay. Here's the truth, or as much of it as I can tell you. Tony Gibson was involved in a scam worked through a series of charity auctions at the gallery where Ms. Hampton was employed. Someone at the gallery had to be involved, and she seemed the obvious suspect."

"*Obvious* isn't always good enough."

A slow anger simmered inside him. If Rojas was content with the obvious, the truth would never come out.

"True," the man admitted. "We don't know how long this was going on. The people involved aren't ones to run to the cops if they think they've been defrauded. More likely to write it off or hit up their insurance company." He shrugged. "You figure they're smart enough to handle fortunes, but seems like they check their business sense at the door when it comes to these fancy society affairs. The Carrington name means something in those circles."

"That'd be Francine Carrington's late husband?"

Rojas nodded. "Carrington had a heart condition. That seems to be common knowledge. He died, and the widow kept up the charities he'd started. Everybody found that admirable. Just lately, though, Carrington's kids from his first marriage have been making noises about the merry widow."

"You knew she came to see Ms. Hampton," he said slowly. "That's why you're here." If the detective was suspicious of a woman in Mrs. Carrington's position, he wouldn't want to raise the wrath of his superiors by leaning on her. "You figured it was safer to lean on Ms. Hampton than on her."

Rojas looked affronted. "Hey, don't tell me it doesn't work the same in your little corner of the world. Some people you just can't jump in and accuse, not if you want to come out with your job intact."

He thought of Keith Morris. "It's better to risk that than to harass an innocent person."

"Well, now, we don't know that Ms. Hampton is innocent, do we? She could be involved, could be the one who faked the pieces. Or maybe she knows something. There has to be a reason why those two women are here together."

The anger was coming to a boil now. It wasn't his case, the sensible side of his mind insisted. It was his jurisdiction, though. His obligation to find the truth.

"You decided Ms. Hampton was the weak link. You figured if you leaned hard enough, she might break."

"It works, more often than not," Rojas said.

"Not when you're leaning on an innocent woman." A woman who deserved better than she'd ever gotten from the law he and Rojas both claimed to represent.

Rojas's brows lifted. "Sounds to me as if you've gotten involved with the woman."

Zach shoved his chair back. "I'm going to get some air. Feel free to use my office." He slammed out before he could say something he'd regret.

The day had slid away while they were arguing. Dusk was drawing in. Unease trickled down his spine.

Caro was safe. Of course she was. Her family would protect her. So why did he have the urge to drive over there, just to be sure?

He shouldn't approach her now, not when she was part of an ongoing investigation conducted by another department. Doing so could cost him. He had to follow the rules on this one.

But maybe following the rules wasn't good enough. His job was a small sacrifice in exchange for the truth. Or for Caroline's safety.

Driven by a need stronger than anything he could explain, he slid into the cruiser and pulled out.

Voices penetrated the darkness, forcing Caroline's eyelids to flutter. She didn't want to wake up. She couldn't. Her head hurt. She wanted to lie here quietly….

But she wasn't in her bed. Hard wooden boards beneath her, not a soft mattress. And the voices—

"You shouldn't have hit her that hard." Francine, but a Francine who sounded different. "We'll never find it without her help."

There was the sound of something heavy sliding along the floor. Her mind began to function. The apartment. She'd been leaving, going back to the house. Now…she opened her eyes a cautious slit.

Now she lay on the barn floor, amid the boxes the movers had brought in this morning. Francine had one of the boxes open, hauling things out and holding them up to examine in the dim light.

"…don't see why I had to hit her at all." It was a voice she struggled to recognize. "You should have offered to help her unpack and sort things out, like any good friend would."

He stepped into the light. Jason Tenley. The photographer. Except that he obviously wasn't. Why was he here with Francine?

"And what if she found it first?" Francine's tone was

waspish. "You should have made sure you had it before you killed Tony."

The words penetrated, and Caro gasped. A tiny sound, but they heard. They were on her in an instant, the man hauling her to a sitting position. The movement sent pain shooting through her head. She struggled and realized her hands were tied behind her back.

"Now we're getting somewhere." Francine leaned over her. "Think, Caroline. Where would Tony have hidden something of value? Something quite small. It has to be here. We've looked everywhere else."

"I don't know what you mean." Which was the truth, and better than any lie she could imagine. "What are you doing, Francine? Who is he?"

Francine didn't bother to answer the questions. She surveyed Caroline for a moment. Then, before Caro could guess her intent, she slapped her.

"Think," she demanded. "Where did he hide it? Help us, or my brother might have to do to you what he did to Tony."

She could only gape at the woman. Her friend. The person she thought she knew. She hadn't known Francine, any more than she'd known Tony.

"Shut up, Francine." The man, Tenley, if that was really his name, smiled pleasantly. "You talk too much."

"It doesn't matter what she hears now." Francine turned on her. "Help us, if you want to go on living. We're not leaving here without it."

They didn't intend to let her live in any event. She knew that as surely as she'd ever known anything. That was what Tenley meant. Francine wouldn't talk so freely in front of her if she was going to let her live.

Tenley intercepted her gaze. "Yes, she really is my sister. Half sister, at least."

"You're not a photographer." Think, keep them talking. Don't sit here and wait for them to kill her.

"Just an honest insurance investigator. Until I ran into my dear sister, and she suggested that there was far more money to be made by skirting the law a little."

Francine gave a low sound that might have been a laugh. "You were never honest, whatever else you were. Stop chatting. We have to find it. If she won't help us—"

The menace in her voice sent a surge of energy through Caro. She wouldn't be a helpless victim. "I'll help you. I know what should be in the boxes. But you have to tell me what I'm looking for."

Francine frowned at her for a moment. Then she came to Caro, bent over and fumbled with the bonds at her wrists. "All right. You're looking for a pill vial. Find it, and you might get to go on living."

"And do be careful, my dear." Jason Tenley waggled the thing that was in his hand. A gun, small and deadly. "I'd hate to have to use this."

No, he wouldn't want to use a gun. They'd want it to look like an accident, like Tony's death. Or even suicide. Widow, depressed over her husband's death, under suspicion herself, decides to end it all. That made sense.

She stumbled to her feet, rubbing her hands together and then grabbing the nearest box. She had to think. *Please, Lord, help me think. Show me what to do. Someone could come looking for me at any moment. Walk in the door and face a man with a gun. Please, help me.*

She felt her control slipping as she pulled things from the box and took a deep breath. *Draw near to*

God, and He will draw near to you. The words seemed to steady her.

Please, Lord. Let me feel Your presence. Show me what to do.

If Zach came—she didn't doubt Zach's ability to handle Tenley. But Zach wouldn't come. Zach thought she was guilty.

Be with me, she prayed again. She opened another box, this one containing clothing, and began feeling carefully in the linings and pockets. Her hands felt stiff and cold.

"Something so small could be anywhere," she said, needing to hear the sound of a voice. "Why do you need it?"

"You don't want to know the answer," Tenley said, leaning against a stack of boxes, the gun drooping.

"What does it matter?" Francine tossed aside a file folder that was probably from Tony's desk. "She's the reason all of this fell apart." She turned on Caro, face twisting with anger. "You never even realized, stupid little idiot. You didn't know what you were saying when you told Garner the one thing that showed I was playing his wealthy friends for suckers."

"I did?" She could only stare at Francine. "I hardly knew Garner. He died the night of that first charity event, right after I came to work…" Her voice trailed off.

Her first event. She hadn't been working at the gallery for more than a few weeks, and she'd been so eager to do well. Garner Carrington, tall, courtly, distinguished, coming into the gallery unexpectedly looking for his wife. He talked to her, probably seeing how nervous she was, and she'd babbled about whatever it was Francine had her working on. He'd already been suspicious, or something she'd said had tipped him off. Francine must already have been substituting fakes for the real donated objects.

"Yes, you." Francine stalked toward her, fury filling her face. "I never planned to harm Garner. I just wanted to make sure I came out of that farce of a marriage set up for life. You're the one who forced the issue."

Horrified, Caro could only stare at her. Garner's heart attack, that very night. Francine, the grieving widow, mourning that if only she'd gone to his bedroom sooner, she'd have found him in time to help.

But she could only be this frantic to find a pill vial if it were somehow evidence that she'd killed him. And the only way it could have come into Tony's possession—

"Tony knew." The words came out before she could suppress them. Tony had known and done nothing.

"Tony knew." Francine shrugged. "We were having a little fling, Tony and I. Nothing serious, but he was coming to the house that night. He was out on the balcony, and he saw me with the pill bottle. He took it. Blackmailed me. If he hadn't gotten so greedy—"

"This is futile." Tenley walked between them. Before Caro could guess his intent, he knocked her to the floor. Pain shot through her. Half-conscious, she felt him pull a rope tight around her wrists and ankles.

"What are you doing?" Francine clawed at his arm. "We have to find it."

"We can't." He shook her off. "We've played around with this stupid plan of yours for too long. The only solution is to burn the place down. The vial will be destroyed, and your little friend with it."

"The police—" Francine began.

"The police don't know a thing," he said shortly. "I'm going to get the gas cans. Here." He handed her the gun. "Make sure she behaves." He stalked toward the door, switching on a penlight as he did. His figure was a dark silhouette in the doorway for an instant, and then he disappeared.

Nearly dark. How long had she been here? They'd come looking for her—Andrea and Rachel would come—

No, Lord. Don't let my sisters walk into this. Keep them safe. Protect them. Protect me. She reached out in longing, in certainty, and felt His presence.

She couldn't be sure how much time passed. She didn't attempt to talk to Francine. She just waited, wrapped in God's love.

Footsteps finally, coming back. A dark figure appeared in the doorway, carrying a flashlight. Awareness shot through her. A bigger, heavier torch than the tiny penlight Tenley had carried, surely.

"About time," Francine said, apparently not noticing anything wrong.

But she would, she'd see— Shoving with her elbows, she pushed herself toward Francine as the fierce beam of the flashlight shot into the woman's eyes. Francine lifted the gun, arm flying up to shield her eyes. Caro raised her bound feet and aimed a frantic kick at Francine's legs.

Deafening shots, flashes of light, loud voices. She didn't know where Francine was. Zach—was that Zach's voice?

The overhead lights went on, blinding her for an instant. Then her vision cleared and she saw Zach, holding Francine in a hard grip. Other men rushing in—

the detectives, local patrolmen. And a moment later Zach was holding her, releasing her bonds, drawing her gently into the safety of his arms.

"Now, you sit quietly here on the bench, and you can watch them work on your new business for a while." Rachel, at her most maternal, guided Caro to a seat on a garden bench that had a view of the barn. "You know what the doctor said."

"He said I should take it easy for a couple of days," Caro pointed out. "Not that you and Grams and Andrea should coddle me for the rest of my life."

Still, she had to admit that it had been healing to spend the past two days doing nothing, floating in a soft cocoon of family concern. She hadn't seen Zach. No detectives had come with questions.

All of the belongings she'd had stored in the barn had been taken away for a police search. Maybe that was just as well. She was ready to concentrate on the future, not the past.

Right now that future was taking shape before her eyes. Rachel had stopped to talk to Tyler, looking very professional with his hard hat and blueprints. Inside the open doors of the barn, she spotted Cal with a crew of Amish carpenters, beginning the work that would transform the barn into the Three Sisters Arts and Crafts Center. It was an ambitious title they'd decided upon. She just hoped she could live up to it.

The quilt would have a place of honor, hung in a glass case inside the entrance, with as much as they knew of its history posted beside it.

That history wouldn't include any mention of

treachery, she'd decided. That could be left for others to argue. She simply wanted to celebrate how the work of a woman's hands had helped lead courageous souls to freedom.

She leaned against the bench, half dreaming in the warm sunshine, and watched as a familiar police cruiser pulled up. Zach. She'd known he'd come at some point. What she didn't know was what they would say to each other.

He came toward her slowly and stood looking down at her. "Any chance you feel up to talking? If so, I'll risk your sister's wrath and sit down."

She gestured to the bench beside her. "Please. I think it's time I stopped floating and found out what's happening."

He sat down next to her, studying her face with that intent gaze. "Is that what you've been doing? Floating?"

"Pretty much," she admitted. "You can tell me. You don't need to hedge around the subject. Did you find the vial?"

He nodded. "Stuffed inside a ski boot, as a matter of fact."

"They were right to be worried. That's one of the first things I'd probably have gotten rid of, since I don't ski."

"That was what motivated all of this, apparently." Zach linked his hands on his knee. "Francine had to find the vial before you did and got curious about why Garner Carrington's medicine was with your husband's things."

"She thought if I believed Tony was still alive, I wouldn't get rid of them." Her brain was starting to work again. Apparently she'd figured some things out while she'd been drifting. Everything Francine had engineered—the love letter, Tony's favorite coffee, the sense someone had been watching her, even sending the safe-deposit key, had one aim—to keep her thinking Tony was alive, so she wouldn't do anything with his belongings until they'd found the evidence.

"That's what her brother claims." Zach wore an expression of distaste. "They're tripping over themselves to blame each other for everything that happened. I guess that'll be for the Santa Fe courts to sort out. They're out of my jurisdiction, anyway."

"They're gone? Don't the detectives want to talk to me?"

"Not at the moment. Rojas seems satisfied that your role was that of an innocent bystander."

"A stupid bystander, you mean." She shook her head. "I can't believe I didn't see anything. I worked on those charity events with Francine and never suspected a thing."

"Francine was one careful lady. Sorting out the truth from the accusations, I'd say she started the scam with help from her brother. Carrington must have already been suspicious the day he spoke with you, though."

She nodded slowly. "I've been thinking about that. At the time, I thought he was just being nice to a new employee, but in light of what happened, he must have been trying to see what I knew. Whatever I told him confirmed his suspicions."

"He let her see that he was on to her. A deadly thing to do with a woman like that. She acted immediately."

"And Tony saw her." The words tasted bitter, but she got them out. "She told me that. She and Tony were having an affair, and he saw what she did. He took the pill bottle and blackmailed her."

Some of the tension in Zach's face eased, as if he was relieved he didn't have to convince her of what Tony had been. "According to the brother, Tony got greedy, and Francine decided he had to go. They thought they'd have plenty of time to search for the vial."

She nodded. "I had a feeling that someone had been in my apartment several times during the couple of weeks after Tony died. I thought it was Decker, the man who threatened me, but it must have been Francine."

"Decker messed up their plans. He scared you into running, and suddenly your belongings were out of reach. Tenley followed you here to keep tabs on you while Francine, playing the devoted friend, found out that most of your things were in a moving truck, making their way slowly east."

"So they had to wait until everything got here to find it," she said. "But I don't understand what happened to Decker. Was he one of the people they scammed?"

"Rojas thinks so. He figures when Decker couldn't get the money out of you, he went to Francine, and she killed him. But neither of them are talking about that, and we may never know."

Maybe it didn't matter whether she knew. Let the law take care of Francine and her brother. But there was one thing she had to come to terms with before she could move forward.

"About Tony." She looked down, realizing she didn't want to see Zach's face when she asked this. "Why? Why did he get involved with me? Why marry me?"

His hands clenched. "Tenley claims Francine told Tony to make sure you weren't suspicious about her husband's death. As to the marriage—well, we know it wasn't the real thing. He may have thought it gave him more leverage over Francine, having you and anything you might remember about Carrington in his pocket, so to speak. Or maybe he just couldn't resist." His voice softened. "People have been known to fall in love. Even the bad guys."

She took a breath, feeling the last of whatever shackled her to Tony falling away. "You're trying to spare my feelings, but you don't need to. I know now it wasn't love with Tony."

"I…" He hesitated, as if not sure what to say. "Is that a good thing?"

She nodded, managing a smile. "I think so. I'd rather know what love isn't, so I can recognize what it is."

Zach touched her hand, very gently, and her breath hitched. Her heart seemed to be fluttering somewhere up in her throat.

"I'm sorry," he said softly. "For the times when I doubted you—"

"Don't." She closed her hand over his. "There were times when I doubted my own sanity. Anyway, you wouldn't be you if you hadn't questioned. You're a man of integrity, and you did what you thought was right."

His fingers moved caressingly on hers. "If there's anything I've learned, it's that when there's a choice between duty and right, God expects me to do what's right." His voice roughened, as if with emotion he was trying hard to control. "Look, I know you're going to need time to come to terms with everything that happened to you. I just hope you'll do it here. I'll be waiting."

She turned to look at him and saw the love shining in his eyes. Her heart melted, and she reached up to touch his cheek, feeling the strong line of bone and the warmth and aliveness of his skin.

"Not so much time," she said softly. "I've stopped running now."

God had brought her back to the place where she belonged—the place He'd been preparing for her all along. And the man He'd intended for her from the beginning.

Zach's arms went around her, and she was home.

* * * * *

Dear Reader,

Thank you for picking up this third story in the Three Sisters Inn series. With this series I come back to my own beautiful rural Pennsylvania and the good, neighborly people who live here, especially that unique group, the Amish.

I really enjoyed writing Caroline's story, maybe because as well as being the artist of the family, she was the youngest of three, as I am. I've tried to convey some of the deep bonds I believe can exist between siblings, which I've certainly experienced in my own life.

I hope you'll let me know how you felt about this story. I've put together a little collection of Pennsylvania Dutch recipes that I'd be happy to share with you—some from my own family, some from friends. You can write to me at Steeple Hill Books, 233 Broadway, Suite 1001, New York, NY 10279, e-mail me at marta@martaperry.com, or visit me on the Web at www.martaperry.com.

Blessings,

Marta Perry

QUESTIONS FOR DISCUSSION

1. Can you understand the conflict between the need to be independent and the longing for family support that drives Caroline? Have you ever struggled to balance two seemingly conflicting needs?

2. Zach is a man of integrity who is driven by his sense of duty. Do you sympathize with his need to do what he feels is the right thing even when it brings him into conflict with people he cares about?

3. Caroline feels that her sisters let her down, even though she tries to look at her experience through adult eyes. Do you have experience of the complicated relationships that can exist between sisters?

4. Caroline's answer to trouble is to leave, but when she comes home she realizes that she's not willing to run away again. Do you think a place or a person can give someone the courage to fight instead of run?

5. Caroline withdrew from God because she felt that He let her down, just as she felt her family did. Emma tells her that if we feel distant from God, it is because we have moved, not God. Do you agree with that? Why?

6. The handcrafts of the Amish and the quilt made by her ancestor move Caroline emotionally in a way she finds difficult to explain. Do you ever have that feeling about objects?

7. Zach has a close relationship with God, but he still has not entirely forgiven himself for his actions. Is there anything that you tend to hold back from God?

8. The scripture verse for this story is a very short one, but it packs some powerful meaning in a few words. Have you found this verse to be true in your life?

9. Caroline finds a community in the other crafters because of their devotion to something she loves. Do you have a hobby or skill that brings you into relationships with people you might otherwise never meet? How can God work in a situation like that?

10. Caroline eventually finds her way back to a relationship with God through the life-threatening events of the story. Do you think we turn to God more readily when times are difficult? Why or why not?

Powerful, engaging stories of romance, adventure and faith set in the past—when life was simpler and faith played a major role in everyday lives.

Turn the page for a sneak preview of
HOMESPUN BRIDE by Jillian Hart.
Love Inspired Historical—love and faith throughout the ages.
A brand-new line from Steeple Hill Books Launching this February!

There was something about the young woman—something he couldn't put his finger on. He'd hardly glanced at her when he'd hauled her from the family sleigh, but now he took a longer look through the veil of falling snow.

For a moment her silhouette, her size and her movements all reminded him of Noelle. How about that. Noelle, his frozen heart reminded him with a painful squeeze, had been his first—and only—love.

It couldn't be her, he reasoned, since she was married and probably a mother by now. She'd be safe in town, living snug in one of the finest houses in the county instead of riding along the country roads in a storm. Still, curiosity nibbled at him, and he plowed through the knee-deep snow. Snow was falling faster now, and yet somehow through the thick downfall his gaze seemed to find her.

She was fragile, a delicate bundle of wool—and snow clung to her hood and scarf and cloak like a shroud, making her tough to see. She'd been just a little bit of a thing when he'd lifted her from the sleigh, and his only thought at the time had been to get both women out of danger. Now something chewed at his memory. He couldn't quite figure out what, but he could feel it in his gut.

The woman was talking on as she unwound her niece's veil. "We were tossed about dreadfully. You're likely bruised and broken from root to stem. I've never been so terrified. All I could do was pray over and over and think of you, my dear." Her words warmed with tenderness. "What a greater nightmare for you."

"We're fine. All's well that ends well," the niece insisted.

Although her voice was muffled by the thick snowfall, his step faltered. There *was* something about her voice, something familiar in the gentle resonance of her alto. Now he could see the top part of her face, due to her loosened scarf. Her eyes—they were a startling, flawless emerald green.

Whoa, there. He'd seen that perfect shade of green before—and long ago. Recognition speared through his midsection, but he already knew she was his Noelle even before the last layer of the scarf fell away from her face.

His Noelle, just as lovely and dear, was now blind and veiled with snow. His first love. The woman he'd spent years and thousands of miles trying to forget. Hard to believe that there she was suddenly right in front of him. He'd heard about the engagement announcement a few years back, and he'd known in returning to live in Angel Falls that he'd run into her eventually.

He just didn't figure it would be so soon and like this.

Seeing her again shouldn't make him feel as if he'd been hit in the chest with a cannonball. The shock was wearing off, he realized, the same as when you received a hard blow. First off, you were too stunned to feel it. Then the pain began to settle in, just a hint, and then rushing in until it was happening inside his rib cage. A pain worse than a broken bone beat through him.

Best get the sleigh righted, the horse hitched back up and the women home. But it was all he could do to turn his back as he took his mustang by the bridle. The palomino pinto gave him a snort and shook his head, sending the snow on his golden mane flying.

I know how you feel, Sunny, Thad thought. Judging by the look of things, it would be a long time until they had a chance to get in out of the cold.

He'd do best to ignore the women, especially Noelle, and to get to the work needin' to be done. He gave the sleigh a shove, but the vehicle was wedged against the snow-covered brush banking the river. Not that he'd put a lot of weight on the Lord overmuch these days, but Thad had to admit it was a close call. Almost eerie how he'd caught them just in time. It did seem providential. Had they gone only a few feet more, gravity would have done the trick and pulled the sleigh straight into the frigid, fast waters of Angel River and plummeted them directly over the tallest falls in the territory.

Thad squeezed his eyes shut. He couldn't stand to think of Noelle tossed into that river, fighting the powerful current along with the ice chunks. There would have been no way to have pulled her from the river in time. Had he been a few minutes slower in coming after them or if Sunny hadn't been so swift, there would have been no way to save her. To fate, to the Lord or to simple chance, he was grateful.

Some tiny measure of tenderness in his chest, like a fire long banked, sputtered to life. His tenderness for her, still there, after so much time and distance. How about that.

Since the black gelding was a tad calmer now that the sound of the train had faded off into the distance, Thad re-hitched him to the sleigh but secured the driving reins to his saddle horn. He used the two horses working together to free the sleigh and get it realigned toward the road.

The older woman looked uncertain about getting back into the vehicle. With the way that black gelding of theirs was twitchy and wild-eyed, he didn't blame her. "Don't worry, ma'am, I'll see you two ladies home."

"Th-that would be very good of you, sir. I'm rather shaken up. I've half a mind to walk the entire mile home, except for my dear niece."

Noelle. He wouldn't let his heart react to her. All that mattered was doing the right thing by her—and that was one thing that hadn't changed. He came around to help the aunt into the sleigh and after she was safely seated, turned toward Noelle. Her scarf had slid down to reveal the curve of her face, the slope of her nose and the rosebud smile of her mouth.

What had happened to her? How had she lost her sight? Sadness filled him for her blindness and for what could have been between them, once. He thought about saying something to her, so she would know who he was, but what good would that do? The past was done and over. Only the emptiness of it remained.

"Thank you so much, sir." She turned toward the sound of his step and smiled in his direction. If she, too, wondered who he was, she gave no real hint of it.

He didn't expect her to. Chances were she hardly remembered him, and if she did, she wouldn't think too well of him. She would never know what good wishes he wanted for her as he took her gloved hand. The layers of wool and leather and sheepskin lining between his hand and hers didn't stop that tiny flame of tenderness for her in his chest from growing a notch.

He looked into her eyes, into Noelle's eyes, the woman he'd loved truly so long ago, knowing she did not recognize him. Could not see him or sense him, even at heart. She smiled at him as if he were the Good Samaritan she thought he was as he helped her settle onto the seat.

Love was an odd thing, he realized as he backed away. Once, their love had been an emotion felt so strong and pure and true that he would have vowed on his very soul that nothing could tarnish nor diminish their bond. But time had done that simply, easily, and they stood now as strangers.

* * * * *

Don't miss this deeply moving
Love Inspired Historical story about a young woman
in 1883 Montana who reunites with an old beau and
soon discovers that love is the greatest blessing of all.

HOMESPUN BRIDE by Jillian Hart available
February 2008.
And also look for THE BRITON by Catherine Palmer,
about a medieval lady who battles for her family
legacy—and finds true love.

REQUEST YOUR FREE BOOKS!

2 FREE RIVETING INSPIRATIONAL NOVELS PLUS 2 FREE MYSTERY GIFTS

Love Inspired®
SUSPENSE

YES! Please send me 2 FREE Love Inspired® Suspense novels and my 2 FREE mystery gifts. After receiving them, if I don't wish to receive any more books, I can return the shipping statement marked "cancel." If I don't cancel, I will receive 4 brand-new novels every month and be billed just $3.99 per book in the U.S. or $4.74 per book in Canada, plus 25¢ shipping and handling per book and applicable taxes, if any*. That's a savings of 20% off the cover price! I understand that accepting the 2 free books and gifts places me under no obligation to buy anything. I can always return a shipment and cancel at any time. Even if I never buy another book from Steeple Hill, the two free books and gifts are mine to keep forever.

123 IDN EL5H 323 IDN ELQH

Name	(PLEASE PRINT)	
Address		Apt. #
City	State/Prov.	Zip/Postal Code

Signature (if under 18, a parent or guardian must sign)

Order online at www.LoveInspiredSuspense.com

Or mail to Steeple Hill Reader Service™:

IN U.S.A.: P.O. Box 1867, Buffalo, NY 14240-1867
IN CANADA: P.O. Box 609, Fort Erie, Ontario L2A 5X3

Not valid to current Love Inspired Suspense subscribers.

Want to try two free books from another series?
Call 1-800-873-8635 or visit www.morefreebooks.com

* Terms and prices subject to change without notice. NY residents add applicable sales tax. Canadian residents will be charged applicable provincial taxes and GST. This offer is limited to one order per household. All orders subject to approval. Credit or debit balances in a customer's account(s) may be offset by any other outstanding balance owed by or to the customer. Please allow 4 to 6 weeks for delivery.

Your Privacy: Steeple Hill is committed to protecting your privacy. Our Privacy Policy is available online at www.eHarlequin.com or upon request from the Reader Service. From time to time we make our lists of customers available to reputable firms who may have a product or service of interest to you. If you would prefer we not share your name and address, please check here. ☐

LISUS07

TITLES AVAILABLE NEXT MONTH

Don't miss these four stories in January

FAMILY IN HIS HEART by Gail Gaymer Martin

Nick Thornton could tell Rona Meyers was a special person, so he'd offered her a much-needed job. And as he got to know her, he couldn't stop wondering if God was offering him a new beginning and a second chance at love.

NEXT DOOR DADDY by Debra Clopton

A Mule Hollow novel

When rancher Nate Talbert prayed for a change to his reclusive life, he got new next-door neighbor Pollyanna McDonald. But the menagerie of pets that she and her son cared for was driving him *crazy*. Could he handle the chaos that surrounded her?

THE DOCTOR'S BRIDE by Patt Marr

Everyone in town was trying to find Dr. Zack Hemingway a wife. Yet the one girl who caught his eye wasn't interested. Why was Chloe Kilgannon hiding from him? This doctor knew it would take some good medicine to get to the heart of the matter.

A SOLDIER'S PROMISE by Cheryl Wyatt

Wings of Refuge

Pararescue jumper Joel Montgomery had the power to make a sick little boy's dream come true. He was determined to follow through even if it meant returning to a place he'd rather forget. And meeting the boy's pretty teacher made his leap of faith doubly worth the price.